20 DAYS OF PLEASURE

BOOK 2 OF THE DAYS OF PLEASURE SERIES

J. L. CAMPBELL

THE WRITERS' SUITE

This is a work of fiction. Names, characters, places, and incidents are products of the author's imagination or are used fictitiously and are not to be construed as real. Any resemblance to actual events, locales, organizations, or persons, living or dead, is entirely coincidental.

Twenty Days of Pleasure by J. L. Campbell Copyright ©2021

The Writers' Suite

Greater Portmore

St. Catherine

Jamaica

Cover Designed by: J.L Woodson: www.woodsoncreativestudio.com

Interior Designed by: Lissa Woodson: www.naleighnakai.com

Editors: Lissa Woodson lissawoodson@aol.com

Betas: Kelsie Maxwell, D.J. Mitchell

DEDICATION

To those who find and nurture true love, despite the odds.

ACKNOWLEDGMENTS

To Naleighna Kai, the Book Whisperer, who is never short of ideas or the energy to see them to completion.

Love and light to the Tribe Called Success, who rally on no matter the height of the mountain to be climbed or the depth of the river to be crossed.

1

S OMEONE WAS WATCHING THEM. The hairs on the back of his neck tingled in response. When they first stepped out of the limousine, Dallas had been relaxed, but as the tour continued he grew more uncomfortable.

Early on, Alicia had felt it, too. He caught her looking around a time or two. As Etienne showed them the sights, she loosened up and was now engrossed in his words. Dallas thought half her fascination was with his eager delivery and lyrical accent.

Alicia slipped her hand into his and brought Dallas back to where they stood.

"Are you serious?" Alicia's eyes sparkled as she addressed the tour guide. Her creamy skin flushed when she turned her attention to Dallas, causing him to brush aside his concern. "Did you know about this?"

The young man, who was in the middle of conducting their private tour of the Luxembourg Garden, had just shared another tidbit. He'd disclosed that in the last six years a Black woman had served as France's Minister of Justice.

"Why doesn't anyone share this kind of interesting information?"

she asked. Gracing the young man, Etienne, with a brilliant smile, she said,

"Tell me more."

Frowning, Dallas scanned the area on the outskirts of the park. A moment ago, they completed that portion of the private walking tour they had booked and were exploring the surrounding streets. While Alicia had been fascinated with the manicured landscape, historic buildings, and sculptures, Dallas was distracted.

Her gentle tug made him move, and when Alicia tipped her head back his smile was reassuring.

"Thank you," she whispered.

His chuckle came readily and with a hint of indulgence. "For what, this time?"

In the two days since they arrived in Paris, she'd shown her gratitude in different ways.

Her eyes glimmered, and he pulled her closer and kissed her temple. "You deserve this experience and so much more."

As her hand slid across his back, she murmured, "You're spoiling me rotten."

"That's what any man with some smarts would do for a woman he wants to call his own." They stopped, and he held both her hands. "For the nth time, this is nothing less than what you're due."

She nodded and gave him another of her sensuous smiles that was sweet at the same time. He slid an arm around her shoulder and walked toward Etienne, who stood a few yards away pretending not to study them. His tiny nod of approval made Dallas' lips twitch. The young man understood what courting was about. He was on the youthful side, but the French had a reputation for being good with the ladies and definitely had the advantage when it came to romance.

Etienne wedged his clipboard under one arm, pointed out a statue, and gave them a rundown on the piece and the artist who created it. They meandered for a few more minutes, until Dallas grew uncomfortable again. He had the urge to end the tour but didn't have a tangible reason. They stood in the middle of the sidewalk, and the familiar buildings confirmed they were close to where they started an hour ago.

When Alicia turned from the statue she'd been looking at and stared beyond him, squinting a little, Dallas made a decision. He pulled out this wallet, slid out a fifty-dollar bill, and gave it to Etienne. "Thank you very much. We're ending the tour here."

The young man hesitated for a few seconds, then folded the money, and it disappeared into his pocket. He tipped his head toward Dallas. "I hope you enjoyed the sights and my service."

"Yes, we did." Alicia smiled, then added, "Thank you."

"Remember to complete the survey the company will send to your email," Etienne said while backing away.

"We will," Dallas responded, then focused on Alicia. He put a hand to her back and guided her across the street to where their driver waited.

A tiny frown marked her smooth forehead when they stepped onto the sidewalk. "It's the oddest thing, but ..."

She didn't continue, and while he waited for what she would say, Dallas' gaze swept their surroundings.

"I feel as if someone was following us but didn't see anyone."

Nodding, he replied, "I felt it too, but you know it's part—" "Of your world," she supplied with a quirk of the lips.

The twenty-minute trip to La Réserve Paris Hotel and Spa—the fivestar luxury hotel where they were staying—passed in silence, except for a question from the driver about whether they enjoyed their outing.

"It was good, thanks," Dallas answered while taking in the scenery and the fact that so many tourists milled about on foot. But then, Paris had many sites worth visiting.

They pulled up in front of the hotel a short while later and approached the entrance hand in hand. A well-dressed female with a purposeful walk came down the sidewalk from the opposite direction. Her gait was like that of a runway model, and Dallas could have been fooled into thinking she had no interest in them except for the way she kept slyly glancing their way.

Just before they came to the hotel entrance the woman, who was a foot away, smiled as if she recognized him and was having a fan-girl moment. Dallas was used to it. His fame as an NBA player followed him to places which no longer surprised him. She grinned, then pulled out a phone and attempted to take pictures of them.

Instinctively, Alicia jerked one hand into the air to cover her face.

He scowled, wanting to yank away the woman's phone, but that might make him look irrational and could get him in trouble. Dallas walked faster to keep pace with Alicia, who he knew was upset. She still wasn't used to having their picture taken everywhere they went. The first time, he could barely keep up with her as she rushed to get away from the young man who'd almost captured them as they exited the Louvre.

Cupping her elbow, he helped her cross the expansive lobby. They were almost at the elevator when someone called his name.

"Mr. Avery, a moment please."

With gentle pressure to Alicia's arm, Dallas stopped her. When he turned with his hand still wrapped around Alicia's elbow and her face buried in his chest, the flash from a camera blinded him for several seconds. Before he could react, Alicia pulled out of his grip and rushed into the elevator.

2

DALLAS' warm hands settled on Alicia's shoulders, and she pulled in a sharp breath. Even after several months, his touch affected her the same way. A shiver of awareness curled to life in her stomach and spread to every nerve ending.

Alicia put her thoughts aside and dredged up a smile. Below them, the hotel grounds spread in several directions, with perfectly manicured grass and rose bushes planted in formation. The floral kaleidoscope, in the cool of the day, contrasted with the conflict raging within. She inhaled deeply and faced Dallas.

"Are you all right?" he asked, searching her eyes.

She nodded and lowered her hand, moving the phone out of sight.

Dallas tipped her chin up with one finger and removed the cellular from her hand. "Have you been looking at the gossip columns again?" "It's hard not to, when ..." She shrugged and avoided his gaze.

He pecked her lips, then murmured, "The only thing that matters right now is what we share. We agreed we'd put the world aside until we get back to the States."

She smiled faintly. "That's kind of challenging when the world refuses to mind its business."

"How about we shower, then have dinner. After that, we'll do whatever you choose."

Alicia's grin was mischievous. "Anything?"

"As long as we don't stray on the wrong side of the law."

Throwing her concerns aside for the moment, she slid both arms up Dallas' chest and around his neck. "What we're doing almost qualifies as being outside of the law."

He gently tapped her nose. "Let's not go there."

"Whether or not we choose to acknowledge it, sometimes I feel like a cradle snatcher."

Laughing, he said, "I think you mean cradle robber, but by no means can you compare me to a baby."

"That's for sure," she said, in a throaty whisper.

Her phone vibrated in his hand, and Dallas glanced at the screen, frowning. When his gaze met hers, he sighed. "Isn't it better for your peace of mind if you don't know what's being said on social media about who I might be dating?"

"I can't help it."

He embraced her, then said, "Our happiness depends on you and me, not what the world thinks, or what's being said in gossip rags, or on the various platforms. Half of what they spread are lies anyway."

"They've managed to stay mostly accurate where your movements are concerned."

"You know they're just speculating on my 'extended vacation', as they're calling it."

"It's disturbing all the same to know you're being followed on all the social media sites each day." She grimaced. "And night."

Dallas shrugged. "I'm used to it because of the games and my following."

His social media pages ranged between five hundred and seven hundred and fifty thousand followers, many of whom had not-so-nice things to say since she'd met him two months ago. Although the comments were not directed at her, Alicia's mind kept straying to the scandals that dogged the men who played for the Dallas Mavericks basketball team.

Last year, one team official was accused of domestic violence by his partner and just weeks ago, a point guard was accused of sexual misconduct with a woman who had been out on several dates with him.

Her mind went back to the glitzy affair, a charity event, where the women in attendance had twittered and simpered while Dallas and Alicia got acquainted. Out of curiosity, they came and went, ensuring they had a closer look at the woman none of them knew, who had won the prize of dinner for two with him.

Alicia imagined that everything she'd ever done and every person she'd ever been associated with would be put under a microscope before the week was out.

She wasn't wrong, but the thing that saved her was the habit of keeping a low profile since her husband's passing. That fact made it hard for the newshounds to track her down.

Because her family leaned on her for everything and took advantage of her generosity as often as possible, she had learned to guard her heart and be careful in her dealings.

Since then, Dallas hadn't blinked an eyelid or acted as if he wanted to back out of their passionate, yet tenuous, relationship. As far as Alicia was concerned, they were charting a somewhat forbidden path for which they didn't have a compass or guide map. Even they didn't know where their journey would take them.

When he approached her just now, she'd been looking at an article titled Cougar Chronicles: Why Some Men Prefer Older Women.

The snarky tone of the article and the speculation over whether a relationship between a male in his prime and a woman his senior would last, wounded Alicia's heart. But she'd known that particular factor would be part of their challenge as a couple.

Dallas circled her waist with one arm. "How about we forget about the world for the rest of this evening?"

She drew a breath to speak, and her phone rang.

Dallas seemed undecided about what to do with the cellular, then sighed and handed it to her.

Alicia understood his reaction because they had agreed not to let their electronic devices interrupt their time together. "Give me a moment," she murmured before putting the cellular to her ear. "Yes, James, what's happening?"

"I need your help."

Her gaze slid to Dallas, who had stepped away and leaned on the wall, frowning at the garden, but she knew it was meant for her.

"What do you need?" she asked her brother.

"Well, uh, Bernice ..."

Alicia sighed at the mention of his wife. The woman's name had the effect of an audio system gone berserk, with feedback that made one's head throb. Her sister-in-law was reckless with money and the main reason her brother didn't own anything. Barely breathing, she waited for him to speak again.

"She's in trouble with the police, and we need bail money."

"And you're calling me because ..."

James knew how she felt about Bernice, plus she hadn't spoken with the family in some time. Only Bernice's belief that the world owed her a living would make Alicia's brother so bold-faced as to make that request.

"If you don't help us, she'll have to spend the next few nights in jail."

That wouldn't be such a bad thing. It would teach her entitled, mischief-making ass a lesson. Alicia didn't ask what she'd done and didn't want to know. When Dallas tipped one brow and stood straight, she said, "I'll have to call you back."

While James sputtered, she looked at her watch. With the seven-hour difference between Paris and Chicago, it was around midnight there now.

Bernice would keep.

3

"HI, Dallas. I'd say fancy seeing you here, but that would be trite."

The woman who interrupted their dinner laid a hand on his back and smiled the way a cheetah would after spotting its next meal. She was an American who was married to a wealthy Frenchman, but that hadn't stopped her from propositioning him since they had met at a fundraiser in New York several years ago.

"Good evening, Kira. It's been a while." Dallas leaned sideways in an exaggerated movement to pick up his water glass, but she didn't take the hint. Her hand remained firmly in place.

Before he could make the introductions, she angled her perfectly made-up face toward Alicia. "And who is this?"

"She is a close friend."

Kira gripped his shoulder hard, then loosened her hold. She gazed at

Alicia with a look that spoke volumes. Her lips curled, then she said,

"Really? That's interesting."

The fake politeness didn't mask the trouble she was trying to cause for him.

"I should hope so." Alicia smiled sweetly. "Otherwise, there would be no point to us being together, now would there?"

The snarky edge to Alicia's voice and the pointed gaze at Kira's hand had the desired effect. Kira clutched her silver purse but didn't move on. Then she said, "I understand, we all need friends ... no matter how old they are."

Alicia didn't shift at the pointed barb. Dallas knew the verbal damage she could do when she tried, so he asked, "Where is Piers?"

Momentary silence surrounded the table before Kira mustered up a nonchalant response.

"At our table." She gestured over her shoulder, then ran one hand through her layered blonde hair. "I had to come over and say hello."

"I appreciate that. It was lovely seeing you." He wished she'd move on, but the woman couldn't seem to take a hint. Alicia was confident and smooth in handling these situations. When provoked, she could be lethal, but he liked knowing she could handle her business without him stepping in.

Kira shrugged as if to say her leaving was his loss, then sauntered away on a cloud of flowery perfume.

"Thank you," he said, meeting Alicia's eyes.

"For what?" She focused on the roasted leg of lamb and herbed potatoes, which she'd been enjoying before Kira interrupted them.

He smiled then. "For being civil when you had every right not to be. We both know she didn't want anything."

"Oh yes, she did." Alicia picked up her wine glass. "She came over here to see who you were with. Mission accomplished."

She sipped a little Chianti, then circled her bottom lip with her tongue. "But like you said, I'm learning to deal with it."

Alicia's gaze settled somewhere over Dallas' shoulder, and he was almost sure she sighed. He laid a hand on top of hers. "Do you want to leave?"

"No, let's salvage what's left of dinner. You're paying a hefty price for this food. Why allow a third party to spoil it?"

He stared into her eyes that flickered with slight annoyance. The constant interruptions wherever they went were frustrating, but so far, she'd dealt with it like a trooper. He had to give her that. What he didn't know was whether he had done enough to make her want to stay with him. Always being in the public view had been part of his life since his career exploded. He'd tried to steer clear of creating waves in the public sphere, but it wasn't always possible. After a few narrow escapes, where women hid in his suite to "surprise" him late at night, then tried to claim he had violated them, Dallas grew careful to the point of obsession and secrecy about his travel arrangements. Part of his precautions included having a hotel staff member comb his suite before he entered.

He hoped Kira's catty comment hadn't hurt Alicia, but he doubted it. Women knew exactly how to land blows neither he nor any other man could fathom, no matter how hard they tried.

Dallas raised his head in time to collide with Alicia's analytical study.

Her attention shifted over his shoulder, which tempted him to question whatever she was looking at, but Alicia only tipped her head to one side. "It's the weirdest thing, to constantly feel as if you're being watched yet not be able to identify what's making you feel that way."

"That's perhaps the hardest part of this life to get used to ... knowing you're always being served to the public on a platter."

To his surprise Alicia grinned, then said, "But when you're as delicious as one Mr. Dallas Avery ..."

He chuckled, and the husky note in his voice reminded him of just how much power this woman had over him, but he doubted that she knew. Dallas stared into her eyes until the back of his neck prickled with awareness.

Someone was watching them, and it wasn't Kira. She had left the restaurant with Piers several minutes ago. The blue-eyed man had barely acknowledged him and even then, he wasn't civil. Dallas wondered what Kira had said or done to affect her husband's mood.

God forbid that Piers should think Dallas was in any way interested in Kira. She had been reputed to have stepped out on Piers a time or two, but that wasn't Dallas' business. He had his own concerns.

After the stunt pulled by the woman in front of the hotel and that newspaper man in disguise in the lobby, whom he'd almost throttled, Dallas' patience was stretched thin. He wasn't one to worry excessively about security, but he believed it would serve him well to pay even more attention to his surroundings or hire a professional security detail.

Their misadventure with that delusional kook in Scotland meant anything was possible. He gripped Alicia's hand and stroked her soft skin, grateful that she was safe and secure with him. If he could arrange it, she'd never be out of his sight for any length of time.

Laughter from diners at a nearby table pulled him from his thoughts. He surveyed the room until a dark-haired man with a hint of gray in his sideburns came into focus. Dallas wasn't acquainted with him, but the light of recognition in the other man's gaze sent alarm shooting through Dallas' brain.

His attention settled on Alicia who had picked up her wine glass.

"Do you mind if I leave you for a moment?" Dallas asked, letting his thumb roam her skin.

She eyed him over the lip of the glass. "As long as it's only a moment, all will be well."

"I promise, that's all it will be," he said, easing away from the table.

The silent exchange with the man a few feet away had Dallas on edge. Since he wouldn't expect to be approached, Dallas seized the opportunity. As he drew closer, the older man twitched like a startled rabbit in the crosshairs of a hunter's rifle.

4

THIS IS what life with Dallas Avery would be like.

Alicia held on to Dallas' hand as the small elevator cabin climbed hundreds of feet into the air. Her heart flipped and settled at the reassuring caress of his thumb on her skin. Soon, they stood at the summit of the Tower in the open air, capped by a star-studded sky.

The view from the Eiffel Tower, or the Iron Lady as the well-known landmark was affectionately called, was stunning. Alicia's eyes barely settled in one place before their guide pointed out another. The Champde-Mar, where it was located, the Notre-Dame cathedral, Place de la Concorde, and other iconic sites she'd had on her radar but hadn't visited.

James' repeated texts were the only disturbance that marred the last few hours. She put her family out of mind and inhaled deeply. The moment she let out her breath, the phone beeped inside her purse. Against her better judgment, she pulled it out. Her brother was now calling. "I'm so sorry," she said to Dallas. "I need to take this call.

Family."

His concerned gaze made Alicia resent her sister-in-law even more.

After moving a few feet to the side, she spoke. "Your wife must be in quite a pickle for you to continue disturbing me for hours on end. Isn't it way past your bedtime?"

"If you had answered, Bernice would have been out of lockup by now."

Alicia wanted to wring her brother's neck. Aside from being Bernice's lackey, she now had him raising money to help her slide out of whatever misdeed had put her in trouble. She drew a calming breath. "Neither you nor Bernice is my responsibility. You're out of order to be tracking me down all hours of the day and night to sort out your problems—"

"You know Bernice. She threatened—"

"I don't care what she threatened." At Dallas' frown in her direction, Alicia lowered her voice. "Nothing on earth can make me shell out money to rescue your good-for-nothing wife. Stop badgering me. Isn't it enough that you're living in my house and that the two of you always find a way to disrupt my life?"

When Dallas walked purposefully in her direction, Alicia tacked on, "I'm sorry, James. I have to go."

Touching her elbow, Dallas said. "You've been gone a while. Is everybody okay?"

Flashing a smile, Alicia walked back toward their guide. "Yes. My brother was calling. His wife is indisposed, but she'll be fine."

Dallas slight frown said he wasn't convinced, but she gave his arm a reassuring squeeze and turned her attention to their guide, who pointed out a landmark in the distance.

The City of Light was a fitting end to a romantic evening after their sumptuous dinner at a gourmet restaurant. They both ate Navarin, a delicious lamb stew served with vegetables, accompanied by glasses of Bordeaux. They had left the tour at dessert, based on her preference. The exercise would be good after eating this late in the evening. Sitting down to dine at half past eight, or later, was the norm in this part of the world, which was fine since they had been out exploring during the day.

Their tour guide gave them the short version of the Tower's

history. Built in two years, it was completed in 1889 and was part of the attraction for the World's Fair. Alicia was amazed at the thought of six million people visiting the Tower each year. But Paris was the place for lovers, so it made sense that people would want to live their dreams by standing inside the impressive monument. Just as they were doing. Dallas was truly a romantic at heart. She was coming to accept that despite whatever she said to him, Dallas knew exactly what he wanted, and what he wanted was her.

The same way her weak-kneed brother and his leech of a wife knew how to find her to drain the life and financial resources from her whenever they were out of their depth. She shut the door on that thought and drew the silk shawl closer around her shoulders.

Dallas studied her with concerned eyes, "Are you cold?"

She linked her arm through his and leaned against him. "No, I'm fine. Who wouldn't be with this beautiful view?"

"Agreed. It's weird that I've been in Paris several times before but never took the time to visit all the usual spots. Business always came first."

"This is a welcome break then."

"It definitely is."

Tipping her head back, she said, "I can't wait to see what else you have planned for our time here."

His mysterious smirk told her Dallas wouldn't give any information away. As her gaze went to the other folks around them, Alicia's mind was a hive of restless thoughts. This time, she wasn't considering what other people would think about their relationship but was more concerned with her own thoughts.

Dallas was perfect in every way that mattered, but she kept going back to what would happen after they went back to the States and had to face reality on their home turf. They weren't a conventional couple, and despite what they thought, their friends and family would have differing views.

"You seem preoccupied."

Dallas' quiet comment pulled Alicia out of her head. She didn't connect with him in case her eyes revealed what she wanted to keep hidden.

With one hand, she waved toward the sky. "Who wouldn't be, with all this to take in?"

Arms folded, he stared at her. "Are you sure that's the only thing you're thinking about?"

"For now." She contemplated the glistening waters of the River Seine then said, "Can I ask you something?"

Gently, Dallas turned her to face him. "By now, you should know there is nothing you can't ask me."

Alicia sucked in her breath and laid both hands on his chest. Tonight, Dallas wore a grey suit that complemented his strapping physique and reminded her why women always chased him.

"I've enjoyed every minute spent with you, but how did you know

I'd love Paris, and what if everything—"

He put a finger to her lips and whispered, "Stop right there. We're not doing the what-ifs." Dallas cupped her face between his hands and kissed her forehead. "You're a wonderful woman and deserve only the best. That is the reason I wanted to make this particular trip, but it isn't only for you. We need this time together to know each other better, the things we like, and figure out how to navigate the things we don't." He gave her a toothy grin. "But just in case you didn't notice, there isn't anything about you that doesn't appeal to me."

Alicia murmured, "I could say the same thing. The view is absolutely amazing."

The lights across the city winked in a dazzling display as far as the eyes could see.

When she looked at Dallas, he said, "And so are you."

His lips were a whisper away, so she closed her eyes and waited, but her desire didn't materialize. "What?" she asked softly, brushing his chiseled lips with one finger.

Dallas gently bit the tip of it. "I'm just blown away by you."

"If you don't stop, my head is going to be as big as this tower."

"I'm only speaking the truth."

The black dress with tiny sequins lining the neckline dipped in the back, and when Dallas laid his warm hand at the base of her spine, Alicia shivered. Her response had nothing to do with the heat or cold. Dallas only had to come near for her hormones to zip into overdrive.

As if he understood what was happening in her brain and body, his fingers slipped under the shawl and followed the channel in the middle of her back.

She drew in a quick breath and cleared her throat. "I don't think that's a good idea."

"What do you mean?" he asked as his fingertips moved in the opposite direction and warmed the curve above her butt.

"That." she said, hoarsely.

With mischief sparkling in his eyes, he said, "I hear and acknowledge that."

She didn't know what he meant until he leaned in closer, and she felt the evidence of his desire. Alicia's heart rate picked up as his warm breath fanned the skin under her ear. "I had one other surprise stop planned for this evening, but I believe it'll keep. Let's head back to the hotel."

5

WITH ALICIA NESTLED SNUGLY in his arms, Dallas didn't want to release her or open his eyes. He trailed soft kisses across her shoulders and down her back. Alicia's luscious skin invited him to continue teasing and caressing her.

She let out a soft moan and spoke, her tone husky. "If you keep doing that, we might not go anywhere, and I'd really like that museum visit you promised me."

Now, he didn't want to leave the comfort or warmth of the bed. He turned Alicia toward him, and she winced. They had made love for much of the night and into daybreak. Although Dallas wanted her as if he hadn't feasted on all her delights, he nibbled her neck, then murmured, "Be like that. I'm switching things up a little, although your wish is my command, but later ..."

Her answering grin was music to his soul. Even freshly awake with disheveled hair, she was breath-taking.

"I just had a thought," he said, dropping another kiss on her shoulder.

"That could be dangerous but tell me anyway."

Meeting her gaze, he said, "We'd make some beautiful babies."

The light in her eyes faded, and she shifted, as if to get out of bed. "I need to go."

When Dallas released her, Alicia rose and grabbed the wrap off the floor. The thin material did nothing to hide her curves and made him want her even more. She flipped her hair over the collar and went swiftly to the bathroom. Dallas rolled onto his back, wondering if he'd missed something or if he was overthinking. Did Alicia just slip out of the room to avoid him? He'd find out soon enough.

The other thing of concern was the calls and texts Alicia had been receiving in the last few days. Although she acted as though undisturbed, every time she looked at her phone, Dallas sensed frustration rising inside her.

In the next moment, his thoughts shifted to the other experiences he planned for their time in Paris. They had a week left, and he intended to wring every drop of pleasure out of their time together.

His conversation with the man who'd been watching them at the restaurant downstairs came to mind, and he frowned. The guy had insisted he'd only been staring at them because they were a striking couple, but Dallas didn't buy it. Something familiar about the ice-gray eyes and crooked smile danced at the edge of Dallas' memory, but he couldn't grasp where he'd seen him before. If he was trailing them, the possibility existed that he'd seen him in a crowd during one of their stops around the city.

The low ping from his phone had him rolling over to pick it up.

"Hey, Katie," he said, "What's happening, lady?"

"Why don't you tell me," she said in a cryptic tone.

His gaze slid to bathroom door. "Now why do I get the feeling you called for a specific reason I don't yet know about?"

"You're usually very private with your business, so I wondered why there's a hint out there as to which hotel you're booked into for the next week."

He shot into a sitting position. "What did you say? Who could have —"

"I don't know, but I'll let you know if and when anything further develops. Please be careful."

"Of course, I will. Keep me updated."

"The minute I know something, you will, too."

The door opened, and Alicia walked back into the room, bringing the scent of cherry blossom and a hint of sandalwood with her. He used a couple of seconds to settle his spirit, then tried to make eye contact, but she avoided his gaze. Standing with her back to him, Alicia unwrapped a bath towel from around her head and combed the wet strands onto her shoulder.

Dallas was conscious that a tinge of awkwardness now stood between them. He wasn't one to back away from dealing with issues when they arose but chose to leave the room sensing it was the right thing to do now.

When he stepped into the shower stall, his mind went to the minute the mood changed. He'd only been half serious, but Alicia had taken his words to heart. His comment wasn't meant to pressure her, and he hoped she hadn't taken it as such. He dried off, applied deodorant, and secured the towel around his waist before going back into the bedroom.

With her hair pinned into a knot, Alicia seemed elegant and aloof. But while she applied moisturizer to her skin, he couldn't help watching. As if his admiration was palpable, her emerald gaze locked on his. Then she blessed him with a faint smile.

"Did my going off at the mouth upset you?" he asked.

"No, love."

"Then why did you walk away? Now I feel as if I need to tap dance around the elephant in the room."

Her mouth opened, but she didn't speak. When she stood, a sigh escaped from her lips. "There's no need. Blame me. Let's just say it might be a sore subject."

"How so?" he asked, before he could stop the words.

Alicia's gaze snapped to his. "If it's sensitive, maybe you should reconsider discussing it at this time."

He frowned as she crossed the room to the closet. This was the first time she'd said what might be construed as harsh words to him.

He'd hit a nerve and wanted to be sure she was all right. "My apologies," he said, "I didn't mean to offend."

"You haven't offended me." She buttoned her pants, then slid her arms into a crisp shirt. He loved the look but had also been looking forward to an intimate breakfast in their room without the distraction of a crowd. Alicia seemed to have the opposite idea. He figured he knew the reason.

Dallas padded to the mirror and wrapped her in his arms. In her ear, he murmured, "I beg to differ. When you can't look me in the eyes that, in itself, conveys more than a thousand words."

"I'm perfectly all right." She turned in his arms and kissed his chin. "There, does that work?"

"If you won't level with me, I guess it will have to do for now." He stepped away and deliberately dropped the towel. "What about breakfast?"

He hid laughter because Alicia didn't know where to look. The glow to her skin was evidence of her discomfort. Spinning to face her, Dallas tipped one brow. "Well?"

In a husky tone, she said, "If you don't put some clothes on ..."

Flashing a grin, he asked, "Is that all you think about?"

She crossed her arms. "Just for that, I think we should go to the museum and then have an early lunch."

"Wait a minute, I did say we were mixing things up a little." Being seated across a table from him was the last thing Alicia would want, but Dallas wasn't playing. He wouldn't pressure her to talk, but he'd spent a fair amount of energy overnight, and his tank needed refilling. "I don't know about you, but I'm starving."

With his lips twitching, he stepped into his boxer briefs and went to the closet for a pair of pants. While he pulled them on, Alicia's stomach growled as if protesting.

They looked at each other and burst out laughing.

He walked over and tipped her chin up for a kiss. His tongue sank into her mouth, simulating what they had done for much of the night. When he pulled away, he wanted nothing more than to get back into the unmade bed.

Alicia's eyes were glazed, and her lips begged for his attention. He swiped a thumb across her chin and studied her face in minute detail.

Then he sighed. "Let's call a truce, shall we?"

"I didn't know we were at war," she whispered.

"We're not, but we need to talk. You know that."

Alicia pulled in her breath and nodded. "Truce."

6

THE EXTENDED MESSAGING session with Katie concerned Dallas. She contacted him by text less than two hours after they spoke. This time, she named the social media account she was following, The Sporting Eye, had promised to update their followers with Dallas Avery's exact location in Paris. What concerned Katie was that the owner of the page had posted the name of another hotel on the same avenue with the sly hint that he was staying a few doors up the street.

Book us into another hotel, he texted. Make it sooner, rather than later.

Her return message came in seconds. On it. Meanwhile I'll turn over some rocks to find out where this is coming from.

Thank you.

His attention returned to the day's outing, which was more to his taste than yesterday's museum trip. Black Paris was not to be missed, and Alicia's interest told Dallas he'd made the right choice. They had briefly visited the Arc de Triomphe and learned of African Americans, including Eugene Bullard, who adopted France as his homeland after being brought over to fight in both World Wars.

While Alicia listened in wonder to Bullard's history—of having served in the French Foreign Legion and being recognized as the first African American military pilot—Dallas racked his brain over who would be intent on putting his private life in the public domain. He could think of a few unhappy souls, but none who knew of his relationship with Alicia. And for now, he wanted to keep things that way.

She was still absorbed with the sights and listened intently while their guide shared that Bullard, who left America to avoid Jim Crow conditions, was eventually made a Knight of the French Legion of Honor.

Dallas remained distracted and eventually excused himself to take a call from his lifelong friend Adrian Hernandez, who was also a basketball star. "Hey, did I say I was off the grid or what?"

Hernandez chuckled. "After the shenanigans that went down in Scotland, I had to check on my main man."

In a calm voice that belied the turmoil inside him, Dallas said, "I appreciate that and everything you did to help us with that situation, but I was serious. Still am. I need this time, without all the interruptions."

"It's like that, huh?"

"Yes, that's the way it is." Dallas turned his face to the sun, grateful for ordinary days. No need for hours in the gym and on the court, muscles burning and his skin dripping with sweat. Despite it being the off-season, he still did a full body work-out every other day to stay in shape.

Watching Alicia as she walked ahead with their guide did his heart good. Tendrils of her soft hair had escaped from the bun at the back of her head and floated on the wind. She raised one arm to clear her vision and the movement tightened the white sundress around her figure. He looked away, distracted. Going by what he knew, he'd never get tired of this woman.

"I don't know why I even asked that." Hernandez's voice interrupted his musing. "It's clear you have it bad for Alicia, and there's the fact that you've never needed the limelight."

"Facts."

"So, as a matter of interest, how are you avoiding the media? There's speculation about why you're under the radar, despite the pictures you're sharing. And, there's been a tweet or two about you being spotted in Paris. Haven't seen any unauthorized pictures yet though."

"Good. I aim to keep it that way."

Alicia stopped in front of a monument, then turned and beckoned to him.

"I have to go." With a soft chuckle, he added, "Remember, don't call me, I'll call you."

"Got it. Over and out. Enjoy."

When he caught up with Alicia, she slid one arm through his and pointed to a gigantic pair of handcuffs and shackles. "That artwork is dedicated to France abolishing the slave trade in the Caribbean." "Want to take a picture?" he asked.

"I don't think so." Slowly, she shook her head. "There's just something about those handcuffs."

Dallas slipped his arm around her, understanding that the artwork might have brought back bad memories from the ordeal in Scotland, when she'd been held prisoner by a deranged man with delusions of grandeur.

"Understood. I shouldn't have suggested it."

"You're good," she said, gripping his fingers as they walked into the shade. "I'm just being silly."

Tipping her chin up, he said, "No, love. Whatever makes you happy, that's what we're going to do. Every. Single. Time. You hear me?"

"Yes, sir."

Her serene smile blessed him, and he sent up a prayer of thanks for their safety.

"So where were we?" he asked.

From a few feet away, their guide, Henri, cleared his throat. "It is time to tell you about the influence of the American artists, who settled in France. James Baldwin, Dr. W.E.B. Dubois, Langston Hughes, and Frederick Douglass, among a host of other famous creatives. As you may know, they came here to avoid racism in America."

As they walked, he spoke of Toussaint L'Ouverture, the man who led the revolt in 1791, which resulted in Haiti being the first black ruled country in the western world.

Alicia shuddered when they came to the Place de la Concorde where thousands were executed by the guillotine during the French Revolution. They continued to the oldest monument, the Luxor Obelisk from Egypt that was erected in 1833. Originally, the obelisk was an astrological tool designed to chart the path of the sun and the stars. "It's a matching pair," their slender guide advised. "The other one still stands at the

Luxor temple in Egypt. It was too expensive to move here."

When Alicia was tired of walking, Dallas summoned a limo, and Henri regaled them with stories about Miles Davis, legendary American jazz musician, and Josephine Baker, who became a French citizen. On the way past Place Josephine Baker, Henri told them that the legendary dancer and jazz singer had starred in a silent film Siren of the Tropics, which made her the first African American to appear in a major motion picture.

With a conspiratorial grin, Henri leaned toward them, "She will have the honor of being only one of five women inducted into the Panthéon for her role in resisting the Nazis in the Second World War."

"Now there's someone who used her influence to do good," Dallas said.

Nodding enthusiastically, Henri gushed, "She was a true patriot and a humanitarian."

"I know someone else who does good quietly," Alicia murmured.

Wearing a slight smile, Dallas tipped his head in acknowledgement. He'd started a foundation for low-income women who suffered from breast cancer, as well as a non-profit to provide meals and school supplies for needy children.

He'd come a long way since childhood, but he was conscious of the many struggles that women faced in raising their offspring. His mother was close to his heart, so choosing to assist women was a no-brainer.

Henri's chatter became background noise as he talked about restaurants around the city that served food from Cameroon, Ethiopia, Senegal, Martinque, and Jamaica. "As you would expect, there are communities formed by people from these places here, including Jamaicans who mainly come as teaching assistants. They have brought their dancehall music, alongside the older roots-reggae that is known to

Parisians."

The buzzing from Alicia's phone pulled Dallas out of his thoughts.

Her sour expression when she looked at the screen told him she didn't want to hear from whoever was trying to make contact. Instead of answering, she muttered and slid the cellular back into her purse.

Dallas opened his mouth to ask if everything was fine, but her stubborn expression made him reconsider intruding on her privacy.

Ten minutes after they finished the day's activities, Dallas helped Alicia from the car in front of the hotel. With his arm around her waist, he made a straight line for the elevator. The doors opened, and Kira and Piers faced them. With little more than a growl in his throat, Piers acknowledged Dallas before brushing past, gripping Kira tightly by the arm.

Dallas wondered what she'd told Piers, but his thoughts froze when Kira flashed him a glare that signaled more than annoyance. When she looked at Alicia, her eyes glittered with spite. As the elevator doors closed, Kira looked over her shoulder with a scornful expression he couldn't miss. Their gazes connected for a second, and if he had to guess, he'd say Kira's was smug.

He was certain Alicia hadn't missed the exchange, but chose not to address it. If she didn't push the issue, he'd let it slide. Kira's reaction wasn't exactly a mystery, but her attitude reeked of someone who was connected to him in a significant way and entitled to his attention.

That bothered him.

7

ALICIA SHOULD HAVE KNOWN she hadn't heard the last from her brother. Not to mention the problem he'd taken on for better or worse. She'd held out on them for another day before wiring money to James. She couldn't imagine what he needed this time. The two calls she missed from him yesterday clearly weren't a big enough hint that she might be avoiding him.

Standing in a corner of the vast gallery, she kept her voice low. "It's curious that I haven't heard from you in ages. And worse, although I gave you the cash, against my better judgement I would add, here you are again."

"I'm sorry to have to bother you so soon, but Bernice ..." He sighed before continuing, "She assaulted someone and—"

"Is this someone different from whoever put her in jail?"

He made a strangled sound in his throat. "Yes, this case was before the bail money incident, so they put her back in for the old case. Arrested her right outside the beauty salon in front of all those chatterboxes."

As if she deserves anything else.

When Dallas raised both brows, Alicia put up one finger to indicate that she'd soon be with him. She waited until an elderly couple moved past her before she said, "I'd tell you that you need to get a handle on your wife, except for the fact that we both know you have no control over that woman."

James didn't contradict her because she was right.

"So, are you going to send the money?" he asked on a hesitant note.

"Tell me why I'd want to do that when Bernice doesn't learn?"

A cluster of young people moved as one body, with no regard for where they were and that they might be disturbing others. Alicia barely heard his words over their chatter.

"She agreed to settle, and if she doesn't come up with the money by tomorrow, she'll stay in jail."

Alicia's decision was made for her when Dallas came toward her. "If I give you this money, it will be the start of never-ending requests for assistance in one form or another. Already, I regret sending that bail money. You'll have to figure this out on your own."

James sputtered, but before he could form a coherent sentence, she ended the call and slid the phone into her purse. Alicia wasn't heartless, but she and Bernice had never liked each other. Her sister-in-law was an ungrateful user and schemer, who hated Alicia with every cell in her meagre body.

This new assault charge was one more strike against her in a long time of bad situations Bernice created because she couldn't keep a civil tongue in her head. Alicia hated to leave her brother hanging, but Bernice's dislike, ingratitude, and open disrespect for James were enough to close her mind to their plight.

"I thought we were leaving technology behind." Dallas slid both hands into his pockets and gave her a quizzical look.

"A family issue came up but since I'm out of the country ..." She shrugged, then gripped his arm as they walked across the well-lit space.

Frowning, he asked, "Is everything okay, babe?"

"Yes, all is well. I'm glad you saved this one for last," Alicia said as they approached their tour guide, who waited for them at the next painting, Starry Night Over the Rhône by Vincent van Gogh. The framed canvas displayed bold splashes of color that captured myriad lights reflecting off water in the nighttime. "Impressive. I've always wanted to see this painting, among others."

Joining his hand around hers, Dallas said, "Making you happy is my pleasure."

The impressive structure of The Musée d'Orsay stole Alicia's breath, and she appreciated the private viewing. Their attendant, a fresh-faced woman, knew her subject and took the time to explain various aspects of the impressionist paintings, which included the works of Monet and Renoir. Alicia had never put this amount of time into viewing such a vast collection of artwork.

Dallas surprised her at every turn. He didn't look like the type who would be interested in strolling through a museum holding hands and asking questions about various pieces. His actions showed her how much was still left to know about the man she had fallen in love with. The revelation pulled her up short. When had she moved from attraction to lust to passion and now love? Was it possible?

Their guide's words faded as Alicia's mind went to their time in Texas and Scotland, plus the shared experiences that brought them to this moment. They now stood in front of a huge clock, and as her thoughts darted to and fro, the woman's words weaved into her consciousness.

"... was built in 1900 and was originally a train station. Over the years ..."

Dallas released her hand and wrapped it around her arm. "Where have you gone?"

She looked up at him, hoping her heart wasn't on display in her eyes. "I was just thinking."

"Do you mind sharing?"

A giggle surprised her. "Have you always been this nosy?"

"Do I have to tell you again that anything concerning you is a source of fascination for me?"

When their guide pointed at the space in front of the clock, Alicia nodded. She wanted to know if they wished to take a photo, which was prohibited everywhere else inside the museum. Alicia handed her the phone and posed next to Dallas, who slipped one arm around her waist. After several pictures, Alicia laid a hand on his chest and focused on his face. Her breath left, sucked out of her in one go, because she was sure the deep emotion in his eyes was reflected in hers.

Now, she was uneasy. Her unhappy marriage, as well as her brother's miserable existence with his wife made her wary. After doing penance for so many years with a man who'd never put her first in anything, being with Dallas was sometimes scary and overwhelming. She used the excuse of collecting the phone to step back.

"What is it, love?" His searching gaze would not let her avoid his question.

"Nothing to worry about."

"The fact that you have to say that tells me there's something I should be concerned about."

Wearing a brilliant smile, she said, "This has been amazing. Where did you say we were going next?"

His steady gaze said he wasn't fooled, but she couldn't explain the sudden shift in her mood. Well, actually, she could.

Love.

That one small word carried so many implications she was not prepared to face. After the tumultuous foster care experience in her childhood, she had married a much older man for security and spent those twenty-odd years unfulfilled. Not to mention unhappy. Like James and his bride from hell.

In one night, Dallas had showed her everything she had been missing, including consideration and kindness she hadn't known could be contained in one person. The man was incredible. And he was all hers. If she'd let him be. If she could trust her feelings. If she could let go of the past and stay fixed on the present and the future.

That was sometimes hard to do with a man with Dallas' fame. Yesterday, with a bare-bones explanation, which she suspected had to do with that nasty bit of work named Kira, Dallas moved them from La Reserve to another exclusive property. He had everything money could buy, except privacy and that sometimes spooked her. Life was hard enough as it was without being forced to live it out loud, but fame was the price Dallas paid for his skills and warm personality. His fans loved him and with that came the need to idolize him by whatever means they found, which mainly included social media, which lately, became the bane of her existence.

While Dallas tipped their host, she stared through the clock at the buildings on the other side of the river Seine. They still had so much to see. What she appreciated most about Dallas on this adventure was the fact that he didn't do things in the prescribed order. They hadn't toured the museum in the usual way but had wandered through the immense building learning about whatever bit of art caught their eyes. Mademoiselle Frith had been most accommodating and gave up early when she realized Dallas was firmly in charge.

The pulsing of the phone next to her hip made Alicia lower her head.

James clearly intended to wear her out, but she wouldn't give in to his desperation. She'd had enough of the two of them. Smirking, she switched off the phone.

One touch of her elbow had Alicia pivoting to face Dallas.

In her ear, he said, "You've going to love what's coming up next."

8

ALICIA'S tight grip on his arm kept Dallas alert. He wasn't certain, but thought someone was following them again. He didn't want to worry Alicia, so he squeezed her fingers while the elevator shot them upward fifty-six floors close to the top of the tower made of glass and steel. The Tour Monparnasse meant an awe-inspiring view of Paris.

"We'll stop in here and get some souvenirs on the way back down," he said, when she opened her eyes.

"You mean there's more to see?" Alicia stared at the clear, blue sky that drew the eyes. The view was stunning. From where they stood, the city sprawled in every direction.

Dallas nodded. "I hear the view of the city is priceless from the top of this building. It's nearly seven hundred feet."

When they emerged on the roof, Alicia's mouth formed a small O as she slowly spun, as if identifying and absorbing the landmarks they had already seen. "Impressive, huh?"

"Definitely." He held up the brochure he carried and glanced over her head. "But the building has been controversial. People believe it's ugly and should never have been approved in the first place. A couple years after it was built, they stopped approving construction of these super structures in the city center."

He chuckled and glanced around the roof but didn't get the sense that they were under observation. "There's an anecdote that says the view of Paris is beautiful because when you're standing in this building you can't see it."

"Really? All of this though ..." She turned to gaze at the city below.

He wanted to grin like a little boy at the pleasure that was plain on her face. Dallas was happy to do this for her. Having Alicia this way had grown on him and experiencing the world at their fingertips was heady. Something he could get used to.

As long as they had interesting places to visit, he could see himself by her side for each new adventure. Now, if only people would let them enjoy each other without him having to always be on alert. But he would do anything to preserve their relationship and the happiness he could soon take for granted.

Standing behind Alicia with both hands around her waist made him contented. "I agree it's awesome."

"Just like you," she said, turning in his arms to look up at him.

He kissed her forehead, then let his lips travel to cover hers. Dallas forgot where he stood as she opened her mouth to let him sample the delights reserved only for him. At least, for now. The thought of anyone else in her life disturbed him. They hadn't discussed future plans, but this time spent with Alicia made him want to look down the road.

He didn't want to scare her off, but he'd always been analytical. Their discussions about business and finance told him that she was also someone who thought at a higher level than most people. As he stared into her eyes, he committed to finding the right time to talk about the things that now weighed on his heart.

She peered at him as if she understood the subtle shift in his mood. Then a smile came to her lips. "It's too lovely a day to be trapped inside your head."

"Agreed, but that really wasn't the case."

"Hmmm."

She didn't believe him, but he wasn't about to get into a meaningless argument. When Alicia had enough of an eyeful, they stopped downstairs in the souvenir shop where she picked up a few trinkets. At her side, staring into a display case of crystal figurines, Dallas was suddenly alert.

Outside the shop window, the same man who'd been studying them at dinner was now watching them again. His lips separated in an awkward smile, and he stalked out of sight. Seeing him was cause for alarm since the move should have rid them of familiar faces. This was a bold move after Dallas' initial approach. He rested a hand on Alicia's shoulder. "Give me a moment, please."

Alicia looked away from the crystal swan she'd been admiring. "All right."

Taking unhurried steps to avoid arousing her suspicion, Dallas walked out of the store and pulled out his phone as if to make a call. Instead, his gaze swept the area as he tried to pinpoint where the man had gone. He hurried past a restaurant with patrons seated outside, sweeping the area as he went. A few feet away, the elevator doors swept toward each other, sealing the man who'd been watching them inside. He debated whether to follow him but decided against it. Alicia would wonder where he'd disappeared to, and if, in fact, the guy was following them, he'd turn up again.

Dallas would be ready.

After a stopover for wine and gougères, he told Alicia they would be returning to the hotel. He ate the last of the small puff pastry made from choux dough and cheese and washed it down with champagne, while she teased him about his appetite.

Dallas didn't answer Alicia's questions, and she didn't pressure him into sharing why they were returning so soon.

"I know enough to expect only the best," she quipped when they stepped into the foyer.

At first, they moved toward the elevator, but he gently steered her down a passage and put a finger to her lips when she frowned. The door of the spa appeared in the distance, and her gaze flicked to his.

"You didn't think we'd come to this place and not get a full-body treatment?"

She laughed then, looking more like a mischievous girl than a mature woman. "With you, nothing is outside the realm of possibility."

Aside from an answering grin, Dallas didn't respond. His mind was on the stranger. He didn't want a repeat of what Alicia had gone through in Scotland. She wasn't a fragile woman, but one abduction was enough to last anyone a lifetime. The possibility of any such thing happening again threatened to steal his joy, but he put his mind firmly in the present as they entered the spa.

Their safety hadn't been threatened, but of course, he'd only be certain of that when he knew why that man kept showing up in their surroundings. He didn't seem threatening, but one never knew.

An elegant hostess, dressed as if she was ready for a day at a corporate office, confirmed their reservation. She then motioned to a uniformed attendant, who led them to private, well-appointed locker rooms. Alicia stepped into the shower stall before slipping into a luxurious robe and comfortable slippers.

While she refreshed herself, another attendant led Dallas to a room with comfortable chairs placed in twos at intervals where those waiting did not have to speak or acknowledge each other. He picked up a glossy lifestyle magazine and flipped through it while he waited.

When Alicia, appeared he stood. "Hey, baby. I take it you're ready?"

They went through a door that opened into a parlor with recessed lights and sparse furnishings. Another corridor led them to a sauna, which their attendant advised would last for fifteen minutes. While she sat with her eyes closed and breathing the warm, moist air, Dallas told her what would come next.

Alicia declined to have the mineral bath, and they were treated to a body scrub that lasted forty-five minutes.

Dallas knew every inch of Alicia's body but being with her in the same space was still a treat. The massage that came next relaxed Dallas so much, he was half asleep. Across from him, Alicia lay with her eyes closed. He loved seeing her that way. As if she didn't have a care in the world. That's how he wanted her, stress-free and ready for any adventure they'd take next. Paris had much more to offer, and he hoped they could finish their time in the city without him having to harm anyone to preserve her peace.

After the facial, hand, and foot treatments, plus time in the salon, Dallas was invigorated. When they headed upstairs, he decided dinner would be a private affair. He'd give Alicia his full attention and show her why they worked as a couple. As well, she'd be safer locked away with him than in the open where either of them might be a target.

Although still unsettled, Dallas hoped their move meant that he could relax a bit because he didn't relish walking around with a security team. That would only draw attention to them when he wanted Alicia to himself. If it became necessary, he'd make the best of that situation. He was nothing, if not flexible. Life had taught him that situations could change in a minute, and with Alicia, he was prepared to pivot to accommodate whatever the future held.

9

T HE WOMAN'S laughter was like broken glass grinding into Alicia's flesh.

Another female snickered. Though heavily accented, her words were clear. "Mon Dieu! He is too much for her."

"Indeed! She will definitely need divine help to manage him. They cannot be together like that because a man like him has plenty of energy to spend."

They laughed again, then turned when Alicia opened the last door in the narrow space and stepped out of the changing room. The two women glanced at each other and shifted on their feet. Their mouths fell open, and the blonde's jaw worked in silence, imitating the desperation of a fish caught on a hook.

"Since he's too much for me,"—Alicia scanned the rail-thin woman from head to feet— "Why don't we go outside and see if he'd prefer to have you?"

She blinked as if she'd just seen an alien and reached down slowly to pick up the dress that fell to the floor.

Moving forward, Alicia continued. "Since you're so confident I need help, why don't we ask him?"

The brunette's eyes widened, and she backed up against the

mirror, as if afraid Alicia would resort to violence. In a breathless whisper she said, "Je suis désolé."

Her apology didn't satisfy Alicia. "You wouldn't be sorry if you were minding your own business in the first place."

She made as if to approach them again, and the two women scuttled out of the changing room. Their hasty retreat was amusing, but Alicia was in no mood to laugh. In fact, she wanted to scream. This. This was what she'd have to put up with if she made it through this stint with Dallas and had any kind of desire for them to stay together beyond this trip.

Even now, she wasn't sure why she agreed to tour Paris with him — aside from the fact that Dallas' presence made her feel safe. She'd done a bit of traveling on her own since her husband's death. Plus, with a family like hers, that took more than they gave, being anywhere other than with them was a bonus.

She leaned against the cool wood paneling, then stood straight. She'd been through worse, so this was nothing in comparison. Her gaze went to the stylish dress she wore. The sheer black and fuchsia material caressed her flesh, and the dress clung to her curves as if it had been especially made for her.

Dallas was several feet away in the high-end boutique waiting for her to model it for him, and here she was having a mini meltdown because of catty women who didn't matter one whit. She pulled her shoulders back and opened the door.

The appreciative light in Dallas' eyes banished the remaining angst. This man appreciated everything about her. Best to focus on that and forget everything else. These ten days in Paris would be over before she knew it, and she was determined to enjoy each moment and make wonderful memories. She spun in the strappy sandals she'd chosen for their outing.

"It is lovely on you, Madame," the saleswoman said with a toothy smile.

"Thank you," Alicia said, but waited for Dallas' verdict.

A decisive nod was his response. "We're definitely getting this dress."

"At this rate, we're going to need two cabs to take us back to the hotel."

With a grin, he pronounced, "You're exaggerating."

She glanced toward the pile of men's and women's clothing next to him. Then her attention strayed to the fuchsia umbrella and raincoat she'd picked out as a memento of this trip, and she held back a smile.

"Right."

For the last hour, they had been inside an exclusive store located on Champs-Élysées. Aside from the ultra-modern décor, the shop had the distinction of carrying over six hundred top-of-the-line clothing labels. As she quipped to Dallas earlier, everything inside was likely to cost an arm, leg, and a kidney. His response had been the usual, a kiss to the forehead and murmured words. "You only live once. Let's enjoy it."

"Wrong," she said. "You only die once. You live every day."

While she tried on a sheath that made her look royal, Dallas settled the bill and arranged for the driver to take their purchases back to the hotel. He took the hassle out of traveling, and she liked not having to worry about everyday arrangements that would have come up if she'd been on this jaunt with anyone else.

They walked out of the store hand in hand and headed to a sidewalk café. Strolling down a busy sidewalk might have been the least exciting aspect of their trip to other women, but she loved being able to do ordinary things with a man who was used to having the best of everything. She was able to unwind because the floppy hat shielded her face and provided protection in case anyone tried to take their picture.

The ham and cheese baguette was delicious, and when she licked mustard from her lips, Dallas stopped chewing and narrowed his eyes.

She raised one eyebrow and smiled in a mysterious way, as if she didn't know the effect of her previous action. "Is something wrong?"

"You've a vixen," he said, wiping his mouth with a napkin. He was about to speak again, when someone intruded.

"Hey, is that Dallas Avery?"

The American accent was immediately recognizable, and Alicia prepared for the interruption.

Four young men wearing baseball caps and carrying backpacks approached them. "Sorry to interrupt, but we couldn't help noticing you." A ginger-haired man with freckled skin beamed as he continued, "I told them who you were, but they didn't believe me. It's great to run into you."

Dallas glanced at Alicia before responding. "It's always good to meet fellow countrymen abroad."

He stood and took a few steps from the umbrella that shielded them to shake hands with each man, as they crowded closer.

"Can we get an autograph?" A slender redhead asked.

After a nod from Dallas, all four scrambled to find paper for him to write on. Knowing he'd probably need it, Alicia retrieved a pen from the purse she carried.

He whispered thanks and turned back to the men, scribbling a few words and his signature on a restaurant menu card, a brochure, and two crumpled receipts. The foursome nearly fell over themselves to tell him thanks. Then the sole Black man in the group said, "I don't want to intrude further, but can we get a picture with you?"

While they arranged themselves and took several shots, Alicia checked her phone. She ignored a message from James, then couldn't help navigating to Dallas' social media account. His manager had uploaded several shots from their outings a couple of days ago. Several pictures she had taken of him were included.

After an appreciative scan, she navigated to the comments. Of course, several females had jokingly stated their wishes to be his traveling companion. One was brazen enough to say what she'd do if she was in Paris with him. Not a moment too soon, Alicia clicked away from his pictures.

Dallas sat and picked up his glass of tonic water. "Thank you."

While he drank, she didn't ask about his words. She knew what they meant. Every time they had been interrupted, she'd been patient.

"There's no need. This is your life."

The reflective tone in her voice caught his attention, and he frowned a little. "And I want you to be a part of it."

To avoid answering, Alicia reached for her iced tea. After a sip or two, she replaced the glass on the small metal table and stared at the storefront across the street.

Dallas said nothing, as if he wanted her to be the one to break the uncomfortable silence. Since she didn't want to spoil what had been a great day so far, she put aside everything that tugged at her heart strings and told him what he wanted to hear. "I'm here with you, aren't

I?"

But his searching gaze told her Dallas was well aware she was hedging.

"Is this your commitment to go wherever I plan to take you next?"

She put a hand to her chest and fiddled with the exquisite yin yang pendant that hung from a 24-karat gold chain. A slow smile came to her lips. Dallas never missed a beat. Even with shadows in his eyes as if he had doubts, his gaze never wavered.

"You're hard to resist when you're this intense." Her breath hitched, then she said, "Would you object if I answered you later?"

Dallas opened his mouth, glanced over her shoulder, and fury filled his eyes. He pushed the chair back and stalked away from the table.

"Give me two minutes."

With her heart knocking against her ribcage, Alicia yelled, "Dallas!" His steps didn't falter. "Two minutes," he called over his shoulder.

Instead of slowing his steps, he broke into a run.

10

AT THE CORNER of the street, Dallas paused then plunged down the sidewalk in pursuit of the man who'd given him the slip days before. He wouldn't escape this time.

The stranger looked over his shoulder, and their eyes met. He bumped into a young woman and stumbled, which allowed Dallas to gain on him. A dozen steps later, Dallas grabbed his shirt sleeve and steered him away from the traffic. With one hand, Dallas pinned him to the brick wall. "Why are you following me?"

His breath came in short gasps while sweat poured down his forehead and he avoided Dallas' gaze. "I'm sure you're mistaken."

"We both know I'm not." Dallas eased back, conscious that people might think he was assaulting the stranger. As a Black man in a foreign country, that might be dangerous to his safety.

The stranger coughed, then cleared his throat while Dallas waited, conscious that Alicia had to be wondering if he'd lost his mind. This was the third time he'd excused himself, for no apparent reason, while in her company.

He looked down the street, where a pair of officers stood. "Maybe we should let them sort this out."

The stranger's gray eyes darkened as his gaze strayed to the policemen, then back to Dallas, who loosened his hold. When he didn't seem inclined to speak, Dallas pulled him closer, tipped his head toward the officers, and ground out, "Let's take a walk."

"That won't be necessary, Mr. Avery." His English was deeply accented, but understandable.

"So, you know my name? I'm sure stalking is against the law." Focused on his shifting eyes, Dallas said, "This is your last chance. What do you want?"

"News," he blurted as a horn blast came from behind them.

Dallas went still, then his head reared back. "Seriously? You follow us all over the city, for what? A stupid story?" "That's not all," he said, shaking his head.

"What else?" Dallas asked through his teeth.

"The paper I work for is doing an exposé. They know you're here and wanted evidence of why you are in Paris. There are rumors ..." He ended as if his explanation made good sense.

Dallas realized then that he was still clutching the guy's shirt. He opened his hand, and the man staggered.

"What is your name and which paper do you work for?"

He stuttered while giving the information, then added, "It is not illegal to gather news on superstars and sportsmen, you know?"

"It is when you cross over into stalking."

Shaking his head, the man who identified himself as Jean-Marc Dupont squawked, "That is not what I was doing, I—"

"We won't argue the point. Maybe we do need to talk with the police, or maybe I'll have my lawyers contact your place of employment. And you."

"Non, non." Dupont gave him an anemic smile. "That will not be necessary. One of our reporters recognized you at the airport while waiting to interview a diplomat and—"

"Your newspaper thought that would be a great opportunity to make a buck off my name, right?"

With a shrug, Dupont asked, "Who can blame them? After the many scandals with the Mavericks and other teams ..."

Dallas searched the man's eyes, sure he caught a glimmer of some hidden knowledge but right now, he was focused on one thing. "Unlock your phone and hand it over."

Dupont's eyebrows rose, his shoulders slumped, and the corners of his mouth drooped, but he reached into his pocket and did as Dallas instructed.

Keeping an eye on him, Dallas navigated to the gallery and deleted the three pictures that captured Alicia and him at the table. He scrolled further and removed another half dozen images of them. The man was good; he'd gotten those images before Dallas was aware of his presence. That angered him all over again.

Stepping back an inch, Dallas pulled out his phone and snapped a photo of Dupont. He'd send it to Katie since she was already looking into who was behind the social media posts and stalking them.

"Here's how this will play out." Dallas handed the cellular back to Dupont and glanced at his watch. The five minutes he'd been away from Alicia were five minutes two long. "You're going to forget you ever knew my name. That you ever saw me. And if there are any pictures of me or my woman in your paper, I'll personally seek you out and make you pay. Even if you did not take the photos. Do you understand?"

Dupont gulped, nodded like a bobble-headed toy, and hustled across the street, oblivious to the screeching cars in his wake. On the other side, he glanced over his shoulder and kept moving.

On his way back to the café, he met Alicia coming toward him with her skirt swirling around her feet. When their eyes connected, his heart smiled, and so did he.

"I'm not the kind to go chasing after any man," Alicia said, "but I wanted to be sure you hadn't landed in anything you couldn't get out of without some help."

"Put it this way, I took care of some unfinished business."

Suspicion clouded her eyes. "Running down the street like a mad man?"

"You wouldn't believe me if I told you what just happened."

"Why don't you try me?"

He slid one arm around her waist and gently nudged her onward. "So, what happened was ..."

Dallas propped his head on one hand and watched Alicia sleeping. He had so much to say to her but instinctively knew it was still too early. Yesterday, he'd wanted to tell her everything that was on his heart but stopped himself. It was enough that she had promised him these ten heavenly days. The only trouble was that their interlude would end soon, and they'd already had enough disruptions.

Katie's early text had disturbed his sleep, but she had good news.

Found the source of the leaks to The Sporting Eye. It's one of your wanna-be groupies. But we knew that.

Her cockeyed emoji with the tongue sticking out made him grin. The news didn't surprise Dallas. He'd suspected what had happened almost from the get-go.

Could be dangerous though.

He waited while Katie continued typing. Access to money, combined with a touch of obsession is a recipe for mischief. You want me to deal with it?

He glanced at Alicia, then sent a message. No, let me do the talking.

One phone call would bring this matter to a close. When it came to Alicia and their privacy, he was serious. He'd shut down this foolishness when he had a moment alone.

Time wasn't something he could afford to waste. Training would resume, and he'd be strapped for time. He wouldn't say he was chasing Alicia. He was past that stage in his life. What he needed was a steady relationship, but she was reluctant to give it serious consideration. Not that he could blame her. Looking at it from her side, he understood how scary it might be to give up her life and throw in her a lot with a man who was so much younger. The long hours away from each other would impact her if she had doubts about what he was doing while he was out of town. Already, she was uncomfortable with what she saw on the internet and heard in the news.

Catfights over his teammates' custody battles, court cases with women claiming to have been sexually assaulted, or not having their children maintained by their fathers. Then there were the scandals with underaged females and incidences of domestic violence. Those women stayed in those troubled relationships because of the lifestyle and money bigtime basketball players could provide. Even at the risk of their self-worth and mental health.

What he owned wouldn't turn Alicia's head because she was established in her own right. She was smart, sexy, and sassy and didn't need him for support. Unlike the women who chased him, hoping for a pay day. Alicia was everything he needed in his life. If only he knew how to convince her they would be a great couple. This interlude was partly intended to do just that. The other half was because he was selfish and wanted her to himself.

She stirred and turned on her side to snuggle into his chest. As she did, Alicia whispered his name, which stirred his first smile of the day.

She made him happy simply by being in his presence. That was something he'd never experienced with another woman. He'd known the moment they met that they were meant for so much more than one dinner.

He ran his fingers gently up and down her arm, unaware of what he was doing.

Alicia's eyes opened, and she whispered, "What time is it?"

"Ten o' clock."

"You shouldn't have let me sleep that long."

"Why not? You deserve it. We did a lot yesterday."

"True." She rubbed her eyes. "What day is it anyway? It's been easy to lose track of the time since we've been moving around so much."

"It's Saturday. We're taking things slow today." He crossed his fingers, hoping her phone notification wouldn't sound off again, the way it had been doing for the last few minutes.

"Does that mean we're staying in or that we'll visit less places today?"

He tapped her nose. "Aside from telling you how to dress, I'm not giving away anything."

"Fine, be like that," she said, as she sniffed and sat up.

They both laughed while she scooted away from him, swung her legs over the edge of the bed, and flounced toward the bathroom that was a showpiece with a 'his and hers' twin set-up and an Olympic-sized Jacuzzi they hadn't taken enough advantage of, yet.

He sat up, reached for his phone, and scrolled until he found the number he wanted. With the phone to his ear, he walked to the window and opened the thick drapes.

"Piers Delalangue speaking. What can I do for you?"

"This is Dallas Avery. We exchanged numbers some time ago at a charity event when you wanted one of your sportswriters to contact me for a feature."

"Ah, yes."

"I'll make this short. My management team traced some information back to your media house. Details on my whereabouts and who I'm with were sent to a certain social media account. I may be a public figure, but that doesn't mean I live my life out in the open."

"And what does that have to do with me?" A ringing phone intervened between them, then Piers continued, "That could have been sent by any member of my staff. Do you know how many people work for me?"

"I'm sure I don't." Dallas straightened and drew his gaze from the silvery glint of the river several miles away. "But what I do know is that if anything else is released about my private life, a lawsuit will follow. Do we understand each other?"

"As long as you stay away from my wife, we're on the same page," Piers snapped.

Dallas smirked, satisfied that Piers had showed his hand. "Trust me, Kira is safe from me. Always has been. Always will be." Piers ended the call without another word.

After resting the phone on the night table, Dallas lay on the luxurious Egyptian cotton sheets, one of the signature features of the hotel. With the issue of keeping his location out of the public domain settled, Dallas emptied his mind and waited for Alicia.

She emerged fifteen minutes later, and after his shower they argued like children over what they would have for breakfast. They fell over laughing when they arrived at the same decision after studying the menu for ten minutes.

When Alicia finally picked up her phone and scrolled through her notifications, she threw her head back and released an audible sigh. "Want to talk about it, babe?" he asked, hoping she'd share whatever had been disrupting her peace. He had no doubt she'd heard from the same person. Again. If he didn't suspect it was a relative, Dallas would have been teed off thinking she was communicating with another man.

She lifted her chin, and a determined light came to her eyes. "No. I can handle it. Another family matter."

"Remember, we're here to relax."

"Yes, thanks. I'm sure it will be sorted out soon."

She avoided the intense look he sent her way by moving to the closet to select an outfit.

Breakfast arrived twenty minutes later, and they sat on the balcony over a hearty meal of eggs, hash browns, bacon, sausages, a half dozen croissants, accompanied by hot and cold beverages. While sipping freshly squeezed orange juice, Alicia watched him with wide eyes.

He paused with a forkful of bacon halfway to his mouth. "You're gawking at me again."

After placing the glass next to her plate, Alicia propped her fist on one jaw. "I can't help it. You eat like a horse."

He gestured to the sausage on her plate. "Since you're playing with your food, may I have that?"

"Of course. We have to keep your strength up." She pushed the plate toward him, then reached for a croissant, which she delicately broke, then bit. All the while, her eyes danced with amusement.

"It's a good thing you're independent. I can't imagine what it would take to keep a man like you satisfied."

He held her gaze as the double meaning to her words dawned on Alicia. Her creamy skin flushed, and he grinned. "You've been doing a fine job so far."

Alicia gave him a cutting look, tempered by a half-smile. "You know exactly what I meant."

His large hand dropped over hers, and she laced their fingers together while her eyes twinkled.

"I'm not admitting nothin'." Dallas chuckled, then added, "But I do want to know something."

"That doesn't sound fair."

He chewed a bit of sausage, then said, "I promise it won't be a hard one this time."

"Go ahead. I'm listening."

She focused on him, then fixed her attention on the beds of roses in bloom below as if she had slipped into the past. Dallas wondered what she was thinking. Sometimes, she had a faraway look that made him wonder what she might have gone through in her marriage. She'd hinted at dark incidents he didn't want to think about. One thing he was sure of, if her husband wasn't already dead, he might have had to do something about him. But the man had done him a good turn by going to his grave. Otherwise, Dallas might not have met Alicia. The thought made him feel bereft. He picked up the cup of hot chocolate and sipped, then placed it back on the saucer.

"You back with me now?" he asked as Alicia met his eyes.

"I'm all yours." Her soft, sensuous voice stirred desire, and he wanted to take her back inside.

Controlling that impulse, he moved in another direction. "Why did you hide from me the other day when I mentioned children?"

11

"YOU AND BERNICE are like canker sores. Extremely painful. Never welcome. But always showing up, nonetheless. What. Do. You. Want."

"There's no need to treat me like this."

"Seriously, James? You continue to harass me despite whatever I say. What would you do in my situation? What do I have to say or do so you'll stop calling?"

He rang again yesterday, but she'd missed it. Her ingrate of a sisterin-law had probably told James not to stop calling until he wrung out of her what she refused to give. The two of them would be desperate by now and scrounging to put the cash together so Bernice could get out of jail. Alicia was likely to be their sole port of call, since nobody with any sense would lend Bernice or James any money. The woman went through the stuff the way water poured through a sieve.

"Just lend us the money."

Here she was, visiting the iconic Notre Dame Cathedral, located on the Ile de la Cité in the middle of the River Seine, but unable to enjoy the tour. The building hadn't been fully restored since the major fire in 2019, but its timeless beauty was extraordinary to behold. She remembered watching the fire raze through the historic building but hadn't visualized standing inside the impressive structure.

Dallas stood with his arms folded, listening to the guide. Other than a sympathetic glance sent her way, he remained silent.

James droned on, and Alicia latched on to the information being shared with Dallas.

"The original building took nearly two hundred years to build, and we are not sure how long the reconstruction might take." The guide pointed to where the 19th-century spire had once stood but was yet to be replaced. "This island was also home to the prison where Marie Antoinette, the last queen before the French Revolution, was held before she was executed."

Alicia dropped back into the telephone conversation with a jolt when James said, "We've already sold some of the furniture, but that's not going to be enough."

With a hand to her forehead, Alicia turned away from Dallas' sharp gaze. "Not content with devaluing my property, because I know your wife is allergic to housework, you're now selling off my stuff?"

"I'm sorry, sis, but we may have to do more if we don't come up with money soon."

"What exactly does that mean?" she asked, seething with anger.

Several voices intruded from his end, and he said, "Sorry, sis. I have to go. Talk later."

"What the hell? Don't you hang up on me, James." But he was gone.

Alicia slid the phone into her purse, willing herself to regain her composure. James had a nerve to be selling her possessions when he'd never owned anything in his life.

After a short exchange with the young man who had been with them for an hour, Dallas took her hand, and they strolled across one of the bridges that sat over the Seine. Despite her unease, Alicia was as enthralled as the other tourists that flocked on both side of the huge structures. Fifteen minutes later, they visited the other island, Ile SaintLouis, where they strolled narrow streets and made their way past a host of boutiques.

Shaking her head, Alicia told Dallas, "We're not visiting any stores. Today, we'll be tourists. Simply enjoying what the city has to offer."

"Do you mind if I ask you something?"

"Not at all," she said, distracted by the tantalizing aroma of warm bread.

"I sense from the snippet of conversation I caught that your family wants something from you." He guided her past a gaggle of young people, then picked up the thread of the conversation. "I've watched you trying not to stress over whatever that is. Why not work out a compromise? Do whatever it is they want and be done with it, so you can enjoy this time?"

She stopped, forcing Dallas to a halt. "Absolutely not."

"That situation has been spoiling this trip for you, but I don't need to tell you that."

He guided her toward a family-owned restaurant and snagged an outdoor table. When he sat facing her, Dallas trailed one finger over her wrist. "I've asked you this question previously, but I must inquire again. Do you want to talk about it?"

His warm gaze and soothing touch weakened her resolve. After analysing him for several moments, she inserted a tinge of amusement in her words. "My brother and his wife, Bernice, are the ones who've been robbing you of the pleasure of my scintillating company, at times."

Chuckling, Dallas said, "You're trying to take me off the scent, but you'd better come straight with me. I'm a good listener. Spill it."

In the interim before their meal arrived, Alicia shared the nature of her problem but cautioned Dallas. "I will not give in to their demands. And don't even think about going behind my back to fix this situation." Grinning like a little boy, Dallas raised both hands, palms out. "No, ma'am. I promise."

"I've dealt with other scenarios like this before. I'll handle this one, too."

"If you need my help—"

"I can always call on you, but this is something I need to handle myself."

They settled over lunch, sharing a wide selection of crackers and cheese, including Gaperon infused with garlic and pepper and BrillatSavarin, a buttery variety they both enjoyed. Alicia had a tiny sample of goat cheese, but Dallas was more adventurous and enjoyed the distinctive flavors.

Their waiter was amused by Alicia's distaste and explained that France produced more than a thousand varieties of cheeses.

"That's all well and good," she said, when he walked away and stopped at another table several feet away. "I'll stay on the safe and narrow and keep to what I know."

Laughing, Dallas slipped another cracker into his mouth. After eating it, he said, "Nothing wrong with that, but life is exciting when you try new experiences."

"It's clear you have no Jamaican friends." Alicia tipped her head when Dallas' eyebrow rose into a questioning arch. "They have a saying that a coward man keeps sounds bones."

He laughed. "What does that mean anyway?"

"You're a smart man." She chided him with a gentle smile. "It means exactly what you think. If you stay on the straight and narrow, you aren't likely to be hurt."

A couple went past them speaking animatedly in French.

His gaze settled on her, and one side of his mouth quirked into a smile. "I'm grateful you didn't feel that way about trying me out."

"Are you a BMW or a pair of shoes?"

"Not at all." His eyes twinkled as he quipped, "Maybe a Jaguar or a Rolls Royce."

She lifted another sliver of cheese from the platter between them. "You have a big head."

"Not at all. I just know my worth."

Alicia nodded in approval. "I can't fault you there."

"Speaking of worth," he said, "we both know our value and what we can expect of each other, but it's the other stuff I need answers on."

Glancing at her plate, he asked, "Are you finished?"
"Just about."
He rose from his seat and helped with her chair. "Let's walk."

For a while, Dallas said nothing, but locked their arms at the elbows as they made their way to a park constructed on a narrow strip of land. Several trees circled a grassy, teardrop-shaped area at one end and funneled into a path lined with metal benches on both sides. Other people sat and stood around talking. The atmosphere was relaxed, and the breeze coming off the river made their stroll pleasant.

A boat went by, packed with tourists sitting at tables on deck.

"That's something we haven't done yet."

Any number of things could happen to a boat with that many people on board. A news clip of the boat with tourists that sank in the Bahamas flashed in her mind. As far as she knew, the legal issues were still being sorted out, with blame being shunted from one entity to the next. "And I'm fine if we don't."

He looked as if he was about to pose a question but took a second glance at the crowded deck and changed his mind. "I hear you."

They stopped at the next bench, and he pulled her down to sit and positioned himself so they faced each other. Stroking the back of her hand with his thumb, Dallas stared at their joined hands. Her heart leapt at the intensity in his gaze. She was so focused on their non-verbal communication that she almost missed his question.

"Are there any dreams and plans you haven't yet achieved?"

Alicia wasn't sure where this question was headed, so she

answered with one of her own. "Why would you ask that, and what about you?"

"I've told you before that nothing about you is boring to me." He waited a beat, then said, "I've achieved more than I dreamed of doing, so right now for me the biggest accomplishment would be a partner to share my life."

His cocked brow said he was waiting to hear her response.

She stared over his shoulder, then at the collar of his polo shirt. "I'm happy where I am, and this time with you has been magical."

As people walked back and forth, she thought about what was lacking in her life.

Love.

The word had come back to haunt her. Dallas made her want more than she'd dared hope for in the last few years. She certainly didn't have many solid relationships that made her believe in happily-ever-afters —especially not in her family. Thinking about them forced Alicia to consider the difference between her brother's toxic relationship with Bernice and the one she had with Dallas.

Everything they shared was far from anything she'd experienced to date. Dallas gave her hope and made her realize that someone to call her own wasn't beyond the realm of possibility. He might not be the ideal age for her, but his maturity was unquestioned.

"So, why won't you give me the time of day when it comes to a discussion about children? I'm not asking you for any kind of commitment. At the time, I was making an observation, but your reaction made me feel as if I'd crossed a line."

Alicia sucked in her breath, released it slowly and remembered where they were. Dallas wasn't asking anything she couldn't answer. She didn't have to make her response more complicated than it needed to be.

"I'm sorry I made you feel that way. It's just that we are not at a place in our ... relationship where I'm comfortable having that talk with you."

He cupped her cheek, frowning. "I respect that, but since we've spent so much time together in the last few weeks, I hoped you were at the point where you felt we could share anything."

"You've been wonderful, and that's where you may want us to be, but I'm ..."

"You're what?" Dallas' voice was like a whip cracking in the silence between them as he withdrew his hand.

"I'm just not ready."

After staring at her while a tic danced next to his eye, Dallas rose and walked away, leaving her wondering if she'd been too frank.

As though on cue, her phone rang. When she fished it out of her purse, James' name flashed across the screen. She put the phone to her ear as Dallas disappeared among the tourists. Although he was upset, she was sure he'd be waiting for her on the other side of the bridge. He was that kind of man.

Sighing, she turned her attention to James. "It's not hard to guess why you're still looking for me."

"I know after the way Bernice has treated you, she's the last person you'd want to help, but—"

"You know what I don't get? Your wife hates me, and yet every time she's in trouble she uses you as a lap dog to play on my sympathy." She stared at the water, sick to her stomach that her brother continued to allow himself to be a pawn. "When are you going to stand on your feet? Isn't it enough she's insinuated that you and I are more than brother and sister? Besides, she's been bold enough to say you don't need me or my assistance. Now, you're selling my stuff."

"I know, sis, and I thank you for bending over backward through the years to help us. You'd be more than justified to kick me to the curb, but I promise—"

"See, this is how she keeps you tied to her skirt tails, treating you like you're some stray animal." Bernice's voice came through the line, grating on Alicia's nerves.

Knowing Bernice was the worst possible person to raise Tori, her brother had been the main instigator in taking away the little girl she loved so much. What galled her more than anything was knowing how they acted after Alicia spent every dime she owned to make Tori whole again.

Whatever sympathy she felt for her brother dried up, and she stiffened her spine. Her heart was heavy, but she could bear so much and no more. Nobody wanted to be taken for a fool, especially by someone as unrepentant and ungracious as her sister-in-law.

"Sis, I—"

"James, don't say another word. I see you found a way to extract her from jail."

"We still need the money to clear—"

"I don't care." A cold draft rose off the water, and she pulled the shawl closer around her body. "You've promised me fifty times already that you wouldn't come begging for money on Bernice's behalf. If she wants to act proud, she should learn to stay out of trouble. Let her go and fleece someone else out of their cash to pay her court fines. Sorry to say ... I take that back. I'm not sorry about putting an end to this stupidity. I'm done."

12

DALLAS COUNTED each second of the next two days. Every moment mattered. A whirlwind tour included everything he thought Alicia would want to see. Still, her family issues intruded on their time. She stood three feet away talking on her cellular, and if she didn't end the connection in another minute, Dallas would do it for her. This wasn't the only thing that bothered him.

As if they were telepathically connected and she sensed his thoughts, Alicia stalked toward him. Her fury was clear in her pinched lips and deep frown.

"What is it, love?" he asked, gripping her shoulders.

Fury mixed with the tears that sprang to her eyes. "My stupid brother just told me that he and his wife put my house up as surety for the bail bonds she owes. Or whatever case she needs to settle."

He hated to see her in pain and didn't want to add to her distress, so Dallas kept his thoughts to himself. Alicia's relatives had been working their way up to this. Weighing his words, he asked, "Will you allow me to help?"

"What are you going to do?"

With his thumb, he swiped away the tear that trickled from the outer corner of one eye. "First, I'll contact my lawyer. Then, we'll pick up where we left off." He tapped her nose. "Stop worrying. Katie will work things out before you know it. You're in no danger of losing your home. Trust me on that." He approached a table at a sidewalk café, helped Alicia into a seat, and got the relevant details from her.

A two-minute discussion with Katie to inform her of what had happened, as well as the nuances involved. Next, he allowed Alicia to speak with her.

"Thank you," Alicia whispered when the call was complete.

Their waiter brought iced tea, which Dallas ordered while Alicia was speaking. She took several sips, then placed her glass on the table. "I really appreciate you. It's a seven-hour difference, so it's after working hours."

"That isn't an issue for Katie." A refreshing swallow of iced tea helped to cool him off. A moment slipped by before he said, "Don't take this the wrong way, but when I make an offer to help, I don't do it lightly. I'd do anything to keep things on an even keel in your world. You mean that much to me, woman."

Alicia brushed the hair away from her face. "I know. It's just that

I'm used to dealing with things in my own way."

"I appreciate that." Dallas shifted the glass between both hands. "But while I'm by your side, allow me to be the man in your life.

Understand?"

Laughter from the table behind them forced Dallas to lean closer to hear Alicia's response.

"I'm not promising any miracles, but know that I don't take you for granted."

"Never for a moment have I ever thought that."

"Good." She rubbed the back of his fingers. "I enjoyed the Latin

Quarter. That was an excellent choice."

For an hour, they had walked through winding old-world streets filled with cafés and bookshops. The area was considered a historic center for education and artistry. Dallas learned that the Quarter got its name because in the Middle Ages students across Europe attended the Sorbonne University to learn Latin.

"I'm beginning to think we need more than ten days to see everything in this charming space alone," Alicia remarked after consulting her brochure and pointing out the section that listed theatres, restaurants, and the open-air bookshops along the Seine.

Despite the discontent rumbling inside him over their unresolved matters, Dallas was patient. "Let's decide where we want to go and do that. We can always return another time."

He allowed that to hang in the air for a moment, but she didn't take the bait.

Pointing to the brochure listing of the famous Shakespeare &

Company Bookshop, Alicia said, "Let's stop there."

He didn't miss the fact that she didn't respond to the suggestion about returning to France. Today was their eighth day in the city, and while they hadn't talked about his reaction to her revelation that she wasn't at the place he thought they were, Dallas hadn't pushed.

When they were alone, the atmosphere between them was now strained, but not enough that they were uncomfortable being in the same room.

Within ten minutes, they were inside the bookstore, and Dallas massaged his jaw while he waited for Alicia to make her selections. She was a complex woman, but he was still willing to do the work to ensure she became his. Alicia was more than worth the effort.

After coming away with a few literary treasures, they visited the Pantheon, where she stood in one place, wowed by the soaring columns, the fine detailing, and the idea of a shrine that housed the country's most famous men, including Louis Braille, the inventor of the Braille reading system for the blind.

He was grateful that for the moment, Alicia had put her troubles aside.

"Did you know about Alexandre Dumas?" she asked when they stood in front of the monument dedicated to him.

Nodding, Dallas answered, "Aside from The Three Musketeers, he wrote ^{The Count of Monte Cristo} and a few other stories and plays."

Her eyes widened, and it was obvious she had important information to share. "But did you know he was Black?"

"I only found that out a few years ago when I stumbled across the information online."

She crossed the marble flooring, tugging at his hand. "This is exciting."

Her enthusiasm was infectious, and he chuckled, thinking about the fact that she even had him interested in viewing blocks of marble inside a mausoleum.

Their next stop was the shrine of St. Genevieve, the patron saint of Paris, inside the Saint-Etienne-du-Mont church. Then they visited the nearby botanical gardens, Jardin des Plantes, which they discovered was started in the 17th century as a place to grow herbs as medication for the royal family.

The extensive acreage was home to a botanical school and over 4,000 species of plants. The dahlias, peonies, and irises greeted them in a riot of vibrant colors. By the time they finished trudging through the rose garden, Dallas was ready to sit at one of the outdoor cafés and sip something cool. But Alicia wasn't done. He humored her when she pleaded to visit the zoo and the natural history museum.

With sparkling eyes, she looked up at him, "Thanks for including this place. It's absolutely beautiful. Do you know this zoo is the second oldest one in the world?"

Wearing a facetious grin, he nodded. "The brochure does say so.

Reading is fundamental."

"Stop teasing me." She poked his side, then spread her arms wide. "This has been so interesting. The last time I visited a zoo was ..." With a shake of the head, she added, "See, I can't even remember."

"Not to worry." Dallas rested an arm around her shoulder. "This will make up for that. As I understand it, many exotic animals live here."

She pointed to their right at an enclosure, "Look, so cute. That's a red panda, according to this information here."

For him, no greater pleasure existed than to watch Alicia enjoying everything around her. She was passionate and submerged herself in each adventure, the same as when they were intimate. He could use some of that loving now, but his thoughts shifted when Alicia interrupted his thoughts. "... last stop the Paleontology Gallery?"

"Sure, one out of four is not a problem," he said, referring to the total number of galleries within the museum of natural history. The displays woke the boy in Dallas as they wandered through the exhibit of both endangered and extinct species. The skeletons of birds, a giant whale, elephants, giraffes, and dinosaurs held him captive, then he joined Alicia near a spotlight on stuffed African creatures that were positioned as though streaming through grasslands on the Mother Continent.

After having their fill, they strolled to Place de la Contrescarpe in the Latin Quarter. The area was reserved for pedestrians, and as they walked the cobblestone streets, Alicia marvelled at the trees lining the pathways. Their leaves had turned various shades of red and orange in response to the fall season. They passed tables lined with fruits for sale, sidewalk cafés, and made their way to a pizzeria with a street-side awning.

Dallas went for a full-house option, topped with cherry tomatoes and slices for Alicia that did not contain pork. She thanked him with an appreciative smile, then watched him devour two slices of the delicious pizza.

"I'm going to say the excitement with my clan and the tour did a little something for your appetite, huh?"

After wiping his lips with a napkin, Dallas replied, "The truth is, my stomach is always at the ready when it's time to eat."

The Shiraz, a flavorful wine made from dark-skinned grapes of the same name, went down well with the meal, and Dallas enjoyed being able to observe Alicia while she delicately consumed her pizza.

She caught him and remarked, "Don't you ever get tired of looking at me?"

"Not in this lifetime, or the next," he murmured.

Casting her eyes toward the plate, she sipped wine then let out a tiny sigh.

He didn't know what the gesture meant, but with only a day and a half to go before they left Paris, he needed to demolish the wall that now stood between them.

13

"THIS IS the first time you've been speechless since we met." Dallas leaned in close and spoke over the noise as the hot air balloon rose from the park located on the bank of the Seine.

"That's because you really went and did it this time," Alicia said, as she clung to the handholds. Dallas had done a private rental, and the only other person on board was their pilot, who instructed them not to lean out to take pictures or rush from one side of the basket to the other, for obvious reasons. He also cautioned them to wear their sunglasses and not become so caught up in getting shots that they missed the pleasure of the ride and the scenes below.

After last night's intimate dinner in their suite and enough love-making to leave her in a daze, Dallas rose early and woke her. "Get up, get up, sleepyhead," he'd coaxed. "There's so much more to see today."

She'd gazed toward the ceiling, but gave in. Especially when she remembered that the man was doing everything in his power to ensure she didn't lose a valuable possession through no fault of her own. They'd eaten more than their fill last night at dinner, so she watched him have breakfast and prepared to have a hearty lunch.

Good thing she hadn't taken a morsel because being so far above the city might have made her queasy if her stomach was full.

"What gave you this idea?" she asked next to his ear. "I'd never have thought of it."

"We've done everything else so ..." With affection in his gaze and an arm around her shoulder, he answered, raising his voice, "I wondered what unexpected, special thing we could do for our last full day here. And this was it."

Alicia took photos of everything that caught her eyes and only paused when Dallas gently squeezed her elbow and presented her with a glass of Sauterne. She didn't ask how he had facilitated that feat, but it wasn't unexpected. They clinked their glasses and stood side by side.

Contentment flowed through her, and Alicia leaned her head against Dallas' chest. Her free arm slid around him, and it was just as well that she couldn't be heard over the burners without shouting. Tears seeped from the corners of her eyes, and she blinked them away. Where had this man been her entire life?

Dallas was young enough to be her son, but for the first time the thought amused her. If she'd met him much earlier, their relationship would have been illegal, and she'd have landed in jail. But make no mistake, he was all man, and his attention and exquisite treatment only raised him higher in her estimation. She said nothing more, but focused on the wispy clouds, trees that appeared to be large dots, and the silvery glint of the Seine below.

When they finally touched down, Dallas held her securely and covered her lips with his. They both jolted slightly, but their kiss was soft and sweet.

"This whole experience has been spectacular."

His response was a sexy smile that made Alicia regret they were so far from their accommodation. Running a finger down his arm, she said, "You're a master planner, so I'm sure you have more items on our agenda for today."

"Actually, I thought we'd spend the rest of the day relaxing. Since we leave on a late flight tomorrow, we'll visit the chocolate museum."

He leaned in to whisper. "Aside from touring the facility and learning new stuff, we'll make chocolate together that we can sample in our suite ... in delicious ways, of course."

The picture that infiltrated her mind, made Alicia smile.

"Our time here wouldn't be complete without us being inside a perfumery," he added.

"Perfume? You're talking my language."

He stretched a hand to help her out of the basket and onto the grassy field, chuckling as he did. "I thought so. I've been thinking about what blend of ingredients could create a scent that perfectly reflects your essence and personality."

Squeezing his fingers, she said, "You've already outdone yourself, so

—"

His eyes danced as he answered, "Lady, you ain't seen nothin' yet."

While their pilot grinned and applauded, they walked the short distance to where their limousine waited, and once inside Alicia leaned against Dallas and rested her eyes as the car rolled smoothly to their destination. In front of the hotel, Dallas assisted her out of the vehicle, and they walked in a leisurely fashion to their suite.

Alicia perched on the side of the bed and opened her purse. She glanced over her shoulder, then dialed James' number. When he answered, she said, "You rang?"

"I don't know what you did and how you were able to do it so quickly, but Bernice is in a state. You blocked us from being able to raise money through the house."

Standing, she glanced at Dallas, who'd been tapping out messages, before moving to the living area. The outrage bubbling inside made it difficult for her to speak in a civil tone. "And that affects me how? You dare to try and sell my property, then have the nerve to ask why I stopped you?"

"If she can't come up with that money, she'll have to serve time," he squawked.

"It seems Bernice has made you hard of hearing. The next time she impersonates me, it would be smarter to engage a realtor who doesn't know me. Not that there will be another opportunity. The two of you better had better think about finding somewhere else to live and how you'll handle the new charges coming against you. I don't..."

She gasped when Dallas gently removed the phone from her hand, ended the call, and slid the cellular into his pocket. "This is our time. Katie is taking care of the problem. Leave it in her capable hands."

Alicia was caught between relief and a sense of anti-climax. "He's going to call back."

"Let him. You won't be answering."

She bit her lips, then a smile broke free. "I like the way you think."

He wriggled his eyebrows. "So do I, lady. So do I."

Gently, he pulled her into the bedroom. When they stood in the center of the room, Alicia asked, "Do we have to go out this evening?"

Dallas stepped out of his shoes and went to the closet. "I was planning to take you dining on the Seine."

She stretched and yawned. "Do you mind if we stay in?"

His shoes landed on the floor of the closet, and Dallas walked back to pull her close and stroke her cheek. Then he murmured against her skin. "I think you like having me all to yourself in the evenings."

"We've been going at a pretty brisk pace since we got here." Her hands slid upward on his chest and linked behind his head. "Can you think of anything better than for us to be together in the privacy of this suite?"

"We'll stay in tonight on one condition."

Fearing what he might say, she loosened her hold. "Which is?"

"That we have a heart to heart."

She shifted, but Dallas gripped her firmly by the waist and spoke against her neck. "We've been tiptoeing around each other for days now."

"Have we?" she asked softly.

He nipped the side of her neck. "You're not a shy woman when it comes to me, although I've surprised you a time or two. I put something out there, and you shut me down. I'm not happy with that."

"Can I shower before we tackle that conversation?"

Dallas took a moment to search her gaze, then nodded.

She stepped away, then extended her hand to him. "Join me?"

They exchanged no more words, but slowly removed their clothing and stepped inside the spacious stall. The water jets hit them from several directions, and, laughing like kids, they clung to each other. Seconds later, their lips were sealed in a deep kiss, with Dallas laving her tongue with his. Without taking his eyes off Alicia, he turned off the tap then lathered her using his bare hands. While he did, she gripped his muscular arms and hummed with pleasure as his nimble fingers slid back and forth over her nipples and teased the pearl shielded deep between her thighs.

Dallas didn't have to ask her to return the favor. She massaged his manhood, moving her hand up and down and teasing the tip with her thumb, but not allowing him to touch her. They were both slick with soap when Dallas opened the spigot again. With their gazes connected, they waited until the water rinsed the shower gel from their skin.

Despite her protest, Dallas lifted Alicia and laid her on the bed. He joined her, using his hands and mouth to show Alicia everything she wouldn't allow him to say. Once protected, he slid deep inside her, lacing his fingers between hers and looking deep into her eyes. After setting the pace, Dallas let her lead, and Alicia locked both thighs around him. With her hips seeking his of their own volition, she ground against him as passion overwhelmed her senses.

Several times, they shuddered and came close to the brink, but Dallas held them back. As he switched position and drove deeper inside her from below, Alicia whimpered in her throat. All sense of time and location disappeared, and perspiration poured from their bodies. Her inner walls gripped him convulsively, and Dallas bucked beneath her. Alicia held on as though clinging for survival while her core throbbed around him, and their coupling drove them to completion. For a while, they were silent.

When he pushed the hair away from Alicia's forehead, she raised her head, drowsy with satisfaction. "I think we'll need the comforter changed. It's sopping wet."

"We'll be fine," Dallas said, nudging her aside to pull the covers back and expose the sheets beneath. He disappeared into the bathroom, then returned with a towel. After wrapping her hair with it, he repositioned Alicia so that she lay facing him.

After pressing a kiss to his chest, she stifled a yawn. "That's until your stomach starts crying out for food."

"Until then, you're mine, and I'm not letting you go."

"Whatever you say."

Tipping her chin to see into her eyes, Dallas shook his head and touched his chest. "You say that so flippantly, as if you don't understand what's going on in here."

With her heart rate inching up by several notches, Alicia licked her lips.

Dallas laid a finger over her mouth. "You've been avoiding giving me any answers, but I know that's because you're afraid of what's happening between us. But I know what I feel about you, and it isn't going away. It's only growing stronger."

When she said nothing, he added, "I'm just waiting for you to catch up."

If only he knew. Now, more than ever, she was certain she loved him. How could she not? Dallas had done more than anyone ever did for her in this life, and she appreciated all his efforts. She simply wasn't ready to jump in with both feet, no matter what her heart said. Maybe with more time, she'd get to where he wanted her to be, but for now she'd remain cautious.

"I understand that, but you can't cajole me into being where you are on this journey."

"Don't you think I know that?" He stared at the contoured swirls in the ceiling. "All I'm doing is laying my intentions out clearly. I want you in my future, and I'm not going to lie about that or pretend otherwise."

"That wasn't supposed to be the deal when we first got together."

"Speak for yourself." He traced her cheek with one finger. "That might not have been your intention when we first connected, but there's no reason the script can't change."

His intensity, accompanied by such meaningful words, would not allow Alicia to look away, and when she couldn't avoid the obvious adoration, she pulled in a deep breath and tried to unravel her thoughts. She pushed at his chest. "I can't think when you're this close."

His victorious smile made her uncomfortable, but he released her without a fight.

She went to the closet and shrugged on a robe, pulling it tight around the waist. Then she faced him, still keeping her distance. "I don't want to feel the way I do about you, but I can't help it."

His lips curved into a triumphant smile, and she put up one hand.

"I'm not saying yes to tying our futures together."

Slowly, she walked back to the bed and crawled onto the mattress to cup his face in both hands. "I'm sorry if that disappoints you, but I'm asking you to be patient with me."

"Your doubts about the chemistry between us never really faded." His breath wafted over her face when he sighed. "So, you don't even have to ask. Not really."

"I promise we can talk about everything after we're back in the States. Let's enjoy this time together, then decide what path we want to take."

At first, he didn't respond, then he nodded. "You've trusted me enough to allow me to take you on this trip, so I thank you. Will you consent to another ten days with me in another location?"

She hesitated, frowning at the doorway. "I do have a life, you know."

"I'm acutely aware of that, and I want to make it one that includes me."

"Persistence must be your middle name," she said, smirking. The truth was, Alicia was at liberty to do whatever she pleased. Another ten days with him wouldn't upset anything, except her equilibrium.

"Most of what I've achieved came with hard work and persistence, so I've learned to pursue whatever I want in this life."

She trailed her fingers over his jaw. "In a relentless but suave way, I might add."

His sexy grin made her heart race, then melt when he said. "So, if that's the case, what is your answer, Lady Alicia?"

With her head nestled against his chest, she sighed. "I won't lie about the fact that you feel like home. That makes me inclined to say yes." Softly, she kissed his cheek. "I also want you to know I'm grateful to you for giving me the space I need to think about us."

Dallas hugged her and whispered in her ear. "That space is about to disappear because I need to make love to you again."

Teasing his ear with tip of her tongue, Alicia asked, "What are you waiting for?"

A NOTE FROM THE AUTHOR

Thanks so much for reading Twenty Days of Pleasure. I hope you've enjoyed this leg of Dallas and Alicia's adventures. Be sure to read the other books in the series and please feel free to share your thoughts in a short review on the platform of your choice. Thanks again. We appreciate you!

ABOUT THE AUTHOR

National Bestselling Author, J.L. Campbell writes in a range of genres. Campbell, who hails from Jamaica, has penned more than forty books. She is a certified editor, and book coach. When she's not writing, Campbell adds to her extensive collection of photos detailing Jamaica's flora and fauna. Visit her on the web at amazon.com/author/jlcampbell or www.joylcampbell.com

Connect with me on all networks.

Sociatap: https://sociatap.com/JL_Campbell/

Newsletter: https://bit.ly/JLCampbellsNewsletter

Some relationships are made in the storm. Real love survives them. Basketball star Dallas Avery has the world in the palm of his hand and a lifetime of happiness or despair within his grasp. For accomplished businesswoman, Alicia Mitchell, love is a double-edged sword wrought with happiness and pain. Business calls the soulmates to Scotland but a new, more treacherous storm is brewing back home. Can their love weather this latest test, or will a crueler fate prevail?

NBA star Dallas Avery has one intention when he visits the most romantic city in the world—win Alicia Mitchell by any means necessary. They relish their time as a couple—free to explore their magnetic connection in Paris and savor the array of pleasures they discover as soul mates.

But family, friends, the media, and society at large, have various opinions about their complicated relationship. Will Dallas and Alicia find a way to stay together, or will the many factors working against them shatter their once-in-a-lifetime romance?

Every end is supposed to be a beginning. After the death of her husband, Alicia Mitchell set herself up financially to embrace freedom and see the world. Then she met a detour. Until NBA basketball star Dallas Avery wrapped his arms around her, Alicia didn't know what it felt like to be cherished. Now he's drawing her focus and shifting her priorities. And Alicia doesn't mind. However, there's a shadow creeping from the edges of her dating history.

Taric Hasan, a man she considered dating until she experienced his dark side, has emerged. Although she once managed to escape him, Taric isn't done with her. He's intent on ending their relationship on his terms ... with her death.

The NBA's sexy and most valuable player Dallas Avery meets the beautiful Alicia Mitchell, who has one thing on her mind: leaving. Their attraction is intense, but the timing is off. Dallas is determined to convince Alicia to give their May-December relationship a chance, but when their romantic trip to the Caribbean gets derailed by them being embroiled in a local family's deadly drama, romance gets put on the back burner.

When an obsessive fan threatens to derail Basketball Superstar Dallas Avery's relationship with the alluring and independent Alicia Mitchell, a trip to Canada comes at the opportune time. The historic sites and chilly landscapes help to stir the growing connection between the couple.

Then a distressed infant is thrust into their care. The teenage mother and her baby are in danger and only trust Dallas and Alicia to help. With the local mob in pursuit and Dallas and Alicia unable to depend on the police, they must flee the country using a historic mode of escape.

Determined to give Alicia Mitchell the love that she longs for, NBA-star Dallas Avery whisks her away on exciting adventures around the world.

Dallas let his heart dictate their journey to Seattle and allows the

Emerald City to work its magic on Alicia. Until civil unrest involving the indigenous people collides with a dirty politician's plans to use city funds to cover personal debts. A chance meeting with Yuma, a tribal chief's son, creates an opportunity for Dallas to make a difference for those whose voices have been silenced. When an altercation with the police develops after Dallas and Alicia assist a homeless woman, Yuma's tribe is forced to shift gears and protect the couple.

Can Dallas keep the love of his life safe, and will the civil unrest drive a permanent wedge between them?

Dallas Avery and Alicia Mitchell are off to Nashville, Tennessee for business and pleasure. Unfortunately, the past returns to haunt the basketball superstar and puts both in imminent danger.

Conway Ackerman has spent the last five years in prison, charged with aggravated stalking of the athlete early in his career. A bitter man with a sordid past, and a psychotic personality, Ackerman has recently been let out of prison and has set a course that will exact the perfect revenge.

While Dallas is aware of the convict's release, he keeps Alicia in the dark. The stage is set for a myriad of adventures, which will extend to the iconic Beale Street in Memphis, but danger is in the midst. A race against time ensues as the couple is tracked from place to place. Will they survive or meet their demise at the hands of a man whose mental state is deadly?

From a romantic picnic in the Southwest to jet-setting around the globe to exotic destinations, Dallas Avery lays the foundation for a longlasting relationship with Alicia Mitchell, brick by brick, beginning with these five words, "Just one more day, baby."

While traveling the romantic countryside from Munich, Germany to Schloss Neuschwanstein, a case of mistaken identity threatens their freedom and possibly their lives. Dallas has faced numerous threats, but

nothing could have prepared him for this experience. A desire to make Alicia's childhood dream come true has evolved into an incredible nightmare.

Dallas and Alicia struggle to learn the new rules of engagement they have been forced to play by. One thing is certain, the NBA player is determined they will not be on the losing end.

Alicia Mitchell, is and was, the only woman Dallas Avery has ever loved. He strives to soothe her fears about their age difference, the unresolved issues of her past, and is determined to make her his forever.

An impromptu trip to Durabia brings more danger to their relationship. Crown Prince Amir sets his sights on Alicia and puts a diabolical plan in motion for her to be secretly brought into the palace where he can have her all to himself. None of them could fathom that a third party would

intervene, and plunge Dallas and Alicia in the middle of a brotherly war.

.

USA TODAY Bestselling Author, Naleighna Kai, tells the dynamic love triangle of a chance encounter that lands wealthy NBA star, Dallas Avery, back in the arms of Alicia, the woman of his dreams. A woman he hasn't seen in years. A woman he soon discovers is his fiancée's long-lost aunt!

But Tori, isn't ready to give up all that she's worked for in their relationship, so she makes him a shocking offer—go through with the wedding and she'll still allow him to be with the one woman he now can't seem to do without. Dallas will get a family, something her aunt can't give him and Tori will have the lifestyle she clamors. And Alicia will embrace the love she's longed for all her life and that had already been in her reach before she disappeared. Everyone will get a little of what they want. . . and maybe a whole lot of what they don't.

The details of the trio's love life play out in the tabloids and on talk shows, making Dallas the center of an NBA scandal. Eventually, the doors slam shut on this open marriage in the making and Dallas is forced to make a choice to end the chaos.

Unfortunately, moving on is easier than it looks and by the time all is said and done, secrets will be revealed, passions will be extinguished, and everyone's lives will be forever changed.

KING OF EVANSTON

"Why do you think she's going to kill him?"

Shaz turned away from the group of teenagers, who were using barbells and didn't need to be distracted. He waited for her answer as his stomach twisted. Camilla Gibson was going to give him a heart attack in no time with her reckless antics.

As he concentrated on the caller, he dabbed his forehead with the towel hanging around his neck.

"Camilla is on her way to

Alderman Bennett's office," Miss Mabel whispered.

"After I told her specifically not to do that." With his free hand, Shaz motioned to the boys. "Continue with your reps. I'll be right back."

The clanging of metal from various gym equipment filled the air as the young men followed his instruction. He stalked to the plate glass door, absently wiping away sweat that poured from his skin. When he addressed Miss Mabel, the owner of the Jamaican restaurant where he ate regularly, he lowered his voice. "I'm in the middle of a workout with the boys and I'm scheduled to have a session with them after—"

"I know they're important," Miss Mabel said, her accent growing deeper as her pitch climbed. "But dis is urgent, too. If ya don' come, I might have to kill ya."

"Why would you want to do that?" he asked, biting back a chuckle. Miss Mabel was always high drama, same as her niece.

"Because my sister might fly over from Jamaica and kill me after Camilla get herself in trouble."

Staring at the red brick building across the street, he said, "You mean more than she's in already?"

"Boy, don't joke at a time like dis." Miss Mabel's voice took on a desperate edge. "Ya comin' or not?"

Despite the way his gut twisted, an involuntary grin lifted his lips as he pictured her scowling. "Don't worry. I'll meet you there in fifteen minutes."

"Ya better make dat ten. The way dat gal behavin', she might be packin'."

The thought chilled his blood.

Camilla, Miss Mabel's niece, was in the U.S. accessing treatment for her daughter, who had a congenital heart condition. The little girl had gone through a series of tests and was yet to be scheduled for surgery. Camilla's visa would expire in just over a month and she didn't want to leave her baby behind and go back to Jamaica, especially since the treatment was not available there. Since Shaz met her four weeks ago, she'd turned his life upside down. This latest episode was a case in point.

He strode back to the teenagers, rubbing the hair on his jaw and chin. "Tajon, you're going to mess around and cause an accident."

The young man anchored the metal disc on the leg machine and raised both hands. "Sorry, Shaz. I got distracted for a second." He pointed to the flat-screen television anchored high on the wall facing them.

The teen doing leg presses grinned. "Distracted, my ass."

A sharp look from Shaz and Chris, who was spotting another teen on the bench press machine, had him mumbling. "Sorry."

Chris Deans, a dark-skinned giant of a man and Shaz's good friend, also volunteered at the youth club they started two years ago. They named it the Evanston Gentlemen's Club and used the facilities, adjacent to the community center, to mentor young men in and around Evanston and Chicago.

As he slid the towel from around his neck, Shaz debated whether he had time for a quick shower. "I have to leave, so you're handling the meeting."

"No problem." Chris tipped his close-shaven head to one side. "Trouble on the horizon?"

"That's what I'm trying to prevent."

In the locker room, Shaz grabbed his bag, then shot in and out of the shower in record time. He shrugged into a long-sleeved white shirt and a pair of dress pants he kept handy in his locker. At five in the evening, they were the only concession he'd make to this errand. Though his career as a lawyer demanded a professional look, he avoided being dressed to the gills as much as he could. He secretly hated suits, but preferred them custom-made for a better fit. Now, he rolled back his sleeves, re-tied his locs, picked up his bag, and left the building.

Five more minutes found him downtown, stepping out of an electric blue Alfa Romeo Stelvio SUV and riding the elevator to Darryl Bennett's office. The man served as an alderman and once wielded power at The Castle, a sprawling estate—a city within itself —where Shaz now had a seat on the board of directors. He and Bennett had had several run-ins, all of them to do with Camilla Gibson. Only God knew what he'd find when he made it to the office.

By Miss Mabel's account, Camilla was threatening to do the alderman bodily harm. After what he'd done, she'd be well within her rights to do so. But that wouldn't help her precarious situation.

If nothing else, the woman had chutzpah. Tall and slender, she was no match for Bennett, a strapping man who stood a few inches taller, and had a lot more to lose if things went south between them.

Bennett's office was elegant, with dark wood panelling and heavy sofas more suited to a living room than a waiting area. Shaz stepped around a table laden with magazines and addressed the alderman's receptionist. He'd barely said two words when Camilla's unmistakable accent hit the airwaves around him. "You're a damn liar. If you think

I'm going to sit around while you ... "

A dozen steps took Shaz to Bennett's office, where he found Camilla stabbing her finger on Bennett's desk, while Miss Mabel clasped both hands to her bosom as if in prayer. When she laid eyes on Shaz, she mouthed, "Thank God, you came."

Standing to one side of Camilla, Shaz gripped her elbow.

She turned wild eyes on him as her nostrils quivered and her lips parted.

With a gentle squeeze to her arm, Shaz murmured, "Now that I'm here, leave this to me, please."

Pointing at Bennett, Camilla spat, "I don't care what arrangement he has with Derrick, he's not getting Ayanna."

Aside from a tic dancing around one of Bennett's eyes, the man didn't move in his seat. He threw a malevolent glare at Camilla before drawing a breath to speak.

Shaz put up a hand to stop him. "Camilla, Miss Mabel, please give me a minute."

After sending the older man a killing look, Camilla swept out with Miss Mabel on her heels. The black ankle-length dress, and her hair pulled into a top knot, highlighted Camilla's regal bearing. At the moment, she might look the part of a queen, but her attitude was far from that of a monarch. If Bennett knew what was good for him, he'd watch himself with this fiery woman.

The second the door closed behind them, Shaz said, "I'm not sure what happened to set this off, but—"

Bennett pointed to the door. "She needs to understand that I've made a legal arrangement with the father of the child. I have—"

"I don't care what you have." Shaz fixed his gaze on Bennett. "What I know is, you'd better put a hold on whatever funny business you have going on with Derrick Porter."

Bennett rose from his seat. "You can't come in here and tell me how to run my show."

"And you can't tell me you're so desperate to solve your family problems, you'd take advantage of someone who's here trying to find solutions for her sick baby."

Eyes wide, Bennett gasped. "You're just saying that. As far as I know

—"

"You don't know anything, so shut up and listen."

Slowly, Bennett lowered himself to the executive chair.

Shaz folded both arms and held Bennett's gaze. "It doesn't matter that she came to your attention the wrong way, Ayanna Porter is not up for adoption. Nor will she be, in this life, or the next. Whatever paperwork or exchange you've done with Porter, consider it null and void."

Moving his head side to side, Bennett smirked. "Life doesn't work like that, Shaz."

"It's Shaz for my friends. Shastra for you. Matter of fact, Mr. Bostwick would be even better."

With both hands splayed on the massive glass-topped desk, Bennett grimaced at the insult. "I don't know what Miss Gibson told you, but my wife and I have a deal with—"

"You clearly didn't hear what I said." Shaz planted his hands on the half-inch-thick glass. "The deal is off."

Read more of this story through the Universal Book Link

King of Evanston

Shaz Bostwick's personal views and business ethics collide when Camilla Gibson walks into his office, seeking his help.

The treatment her daughter needs is available in Chicago, but Camilla is almost out of time and has several issues working against her. Raised as an immigrant, Shaz knows the heartache of family separation firsthand.

In a race against the clock and the authorities, he calls in favors but receives a disturbing offer. Let baby Ayanna slip through the cracks in exchange for a handsome reward. Fed up with politicians and businessmen with too much money and too little scruples, Shaz and his fellow Kings of the Castle band together to stem the flow of illegal adoptions, while they solve the mystery of who wants their mentor dead.

Camilla Gibson has traveled the world in her capacity as an adventurer, sometime model, and blogging celebrity. In her eyes, the charming, but tough lawyer is her last resort before deportation. Shaz is smart and tenacious, with renowned negotiating skills and a reputation for making a way when there seems to be none.

If she can get past the biggest crisis in her life, then maybe the spark of attraction that sizzles between them will develop into something magical.

KNIGHT OF PARADISE ISLAND

"Did you say someone's missing in Durabia?" Ryan walked around the desk and settled into the leather executive chair, moving his phone from one ear to the other. "I'm in the office now and switching over to the chat."

"What are you doing at work on a Sunday morning?" his cousin, Shaz, asked.

"The same reason you're sitting in your office until Camilla drags you away from that desk." He opened the laptop, and Shaz's face appeared on the screen.

"Are you putting on weight or

something, cuz? What's Camilla feeding you?"

Shaz snorted. "You're the one who looks like you gained about ten pounds since we last spoke."

"Whatever, man." Ryan snickered because the entire family knew

Shaz could eat everybody else under the table. And that meant e-verybod-y.

"So, back to business," Shaz said. "Aziza is missing."

"Wait a minute, did you say Aziza?"

"You getting hard of hearing, man?" Shaz sounded testy.

Ryan's chest tightened painfully, and he had to clear his throat to speak. "That's not possible."

On Thursday, he spent over two hours on a video chat with Aziza. They ended the call when she started falling asleep over the laptop. The two of them had been following that ritual since she left the Bahamas two weeks ago. She contacted him when she landed in Evanston and again, when she found out her brother was suffering with kidney stones.

The last time he spoke with her was on Friday while she was getting ready to go out with her co-workers. The only reason he hadn't called last night was because of what turned out to be a non-emergency that involved a missing guest. The middle-aged man had turned up disheveled and hung over after a day and night in Nassau. With the eight-hour time difference, he didn't want to disturb Aziza's rest. Now, Ryan knew he should have done so. He'd have been aware of her disappearance earlier.

"Is there something you're not telling me," Shaz asked, his brows elevated.

"Yeah, Aziza and I … let me put it this way. We're a lot more than friends."

Shaz's eyebrows met as he said, "Dang. You've kept that close to your chest, but then you've always been secretive."

"No more than you." Ryan headed him back to the present business, which had his stomach doing drunken somersaults. "When exactly d'you think she went missing and how d'you know that for a fact?"

"Her parents contacted me fifteen minutes ago. Yesterday was Miss Constance's birthday. She and Aziza are close. She said she'd never miss her birthday." Shaz let out a deep breath. "Her mother was in a state after she called the hotel where Aziza works. They told Miss Constance she didn't turn up for work this morning. Her father had to finish up the call with me."

"Does her brother know?"

"His wife just had a baby, plus he's dealing with his own medical issues. Drake can't be out of range at this time."

"Understood."

"There's some other suspicious activity over there that needs our attention. Missing women are involved, so …" Shaz laced his fingers together and met Ryan's eyes. "I'm asking you to go."

This hadn't been the first time Shaz hinted that he had a special assignment for Ryan, given his five-year stint with the Criminal Investigation Department of the Royal Bahamas Police Force. After reconnecting with Aziza months ago, Ryan had stayed busy with hotel business, as well as expanding the reach of Bostwick Security in the Caribbean. They were in the middle of business negotiations that needed Ryan's input. Now this.

"I figured," he said, sucking in his breath.

Getting away would be challenging, especially since he'd taken time off to be with Aziza. Good thing the director of security at the hotel was his friend. Plus, his brother Myles was more than competent. The two of them ran the security firm and also took on specialized jobs, depending on the needs of their clients.

At thirty-five, Myles was three years older and also in a steady relationship. He was level-headed and wouldn't mind doing double duty while Ryan was out of the country. Ryan's biggest challenge would be those contracts he'd been in the middle of preparing that were yet to be finalized and sent to their lawyers.

"Great. The Kings and I plan to get together within the hour. When we convene at The Castle, we'll set up a video connection to bring you into the meeting."

"Sounds good. In the meantime, I'll talk to Roger Blythe, an extractor who will give me some guidance on navigating through this minefield. He's been everywhere on the map. Then, I'll look at what flights are available."

Shaz nodded and glanced to his left. A smile lightened his serious expression.

"Daddy-Shaz."

His daughter's head popped up behind the desk and a second later, she wriggled between him and the desk and climbed onto his lap. The little girl propped her elbows on the desk and waved at the screen, "Hi, Unca. Where are you?"

"Hey, Ayanna." Ryan wriggled his fingers at the charmer Shaz had adopted when he married her mother. "I'm in the Bahamas."

When he tipped one eyebrow, Shaz chuckled. "When you have a dozen or more uncles, every man other than me gets that tag. Plus, the others travel so much, she understands that screen time means you're not in Wilmette."

As Camilla's distended stomach appeared on screen before the rest of her, Ayanna scrambled to his other side to escape. "Little girl, I'm not playing with you," she said.

"Hey, Camilla."

She focused on the screen, then laid a hand on her belly. "Hey yourself. Everything good?"

Her words brought back the heavy matter Shaz dropped on him.

"Yeah, we're fine over here."

"Talk to you later," she said, and guided Ayanna to the floor. "Come baby, let Daddy get back to what he was doing."

Ryan focused on the legal pad where he'd jotted notes for the report he was about to write on the lost-and-found guest. When he looked up,

Shaz said, "Don't go anywhere."

Ryan nodded, already planning his next steps. He'd have to advise the hotel that he'd be away, perhaps for an indefinite period.

Knight of Paradise Island

Someone is killing women and the villain's next target strikes too close to the Kingdom of Durabia.

Dorian "Ryan" Bostwick is a protector and he's one of the best in the business. When a King of the Castle assigns him to find his former lover, Aziza, he stumbles upon a deadly underworld operating close to the Durabian border.

Aziza Hampton had just rekindled her love affair with Ryan when a night out with friends ends in her kidnapping. Alone and scared, she must find a way to escape her captor and reunite with her lover.

In a race against time, Ryan and the Kings of the Castle follow ominous clues into the underbelly of a system designed to take advantage of the vulnerable. Failure isn't an option and Ryan will rain down hell on earth to save the woman of his heart.

Read more of this story through the Universal Book Link

FOREVER MINE

"Somehow, we didn't realize the room was double-booked," the reservation agent said. Two spots of color flushed the blonde's cheeks, and she avoided looking directly at me when she

added, "I'm really sorry, Miss Young."

She had my sympathy, but I needed solutions.

"That doesn't help my situation," I said, pushing the hair off my forehead.

The man standing next to me put away his cell phone, which pinged a moment ago. My gaze shot to his face, and he looked at me through a hank of black hair. Light-brown streaks threaded through the strands and the

tips seemed to have been bleached by the sun.

His eyes were a startling shade, which shifted from dark to midnight blue as he looked at me. Perhaps it was the hair hanging over one eye, and covering half his face, which gave that impression. I wanted to move the hair out of the way, but it didn't seem to bother him.

His lips quirked, in what might have been a half-smile, before the woman behind the counter spoke and captured his attention.

It was then I noticed his beard. I wasn't fond of them, but the dense stubble on his face gave him a bohemian air that reminded me of sun, sea, and sand. Island breezes, exotic drinks, and warm nights on the beach also came to mind. I put my thoughts down to me being intrigued by an attractive man. That hadn't been the case for some time.

My flight of fancy almost made me smile when I looked at the hotel employee, but I suppressed the urge. She would have thought I was deranged if I grinned without an obvious reason, especially given the challenge facing all three of us. On the periphery of my vision, a herd of people moved toward the check-in counter.

The guy's phone pinged again, and he got it out and looked at the screen. He sighed and dropped it into his pocket.

"Tell you what," he said, tipping his chin toward me. "Give her the room, then try to find me something. The hotel messed up. You need to fix this."

His husky voice sent a shiver down the back of my neck. For me, that was an alien reaction. I stiffened my spine and put it down to being out of sorts because of my current plight.

The woman behind the counter dipped her head toward the screen in front of her. When she looked up, she said, "Give me a moment please. I'll be right back."

His nod was curt, and he muttered as he shoved a hand into his pocket.

The phone had summoned him again. Whatever he had going on seemed to be urgent, which reminded me I'd be in a pickle if I didn't get this room.

I hated travelling. Seriously hated it. Nothing ever seemed to go according to plan. If one thing didn't go bad, it was another. First, the travel agent couldn't get me on the same flight as the graphic artists I was supposed to be supervising. This was their first trip abroad and the two of them were giddy as hell. Then, I'd been put on standby by the hotel hosting the animation conference. They contacted us days ago to say they had a room available, and now this.

Nothing out of the ordinary happened on the flight from Jamaica to Miami, but my luggage suffered. My suitcase had a puncture wound, and the fabric was ripped. It wasn't a major deal, but it annoyed me. Maybe because I didn't want to be in Miami in the first place. My life was in Kingston and traveling hadn't been part of the deal when I started working with Charstat Animation Studio.

Things had changed since I took the job a year ago. In between new projects being added to the studio's workload, and meetings with clients, I'd been off the island three times in the last nine months.

The man next to me huffed when his phone rang. He swore, gave me an apologetic glance, and put the cellular to his ear. "Look, Lucy, how many more times do I have to tell you to stop this?"

He moved a few steps away, hunched his shoulders, and lowered his voice.

The people behind me shuffled and a chorus of mumbles rose.

I understood their impatience, but it wasn't my fault they hadn't been checked in as yet. The lobby was crowded, and I guessed that aside from the animation conference, the hotel was booked solid with other guests.

My cell phone buzzed, and I took it out of my handbag.

Mom had sent a message. Did you get there okay?

I wrote back. Yes, I'm about to check in. Sorry. Should have texted when I got here.

I added a heart emoticon and grinned when she sent one blowing a kiss. My mother wasn't like most sixty-something women. Sometimes, I thought she knew more than I did about messaging apps and social media platforms.

Since I had the phone out, I checked my email. Having done that, I responded to a message from Joey—one of the young men on the trip— who finally answered the text I sent him when I landed. In a few words, he let me know he and Pete arrived safely and were in their room. I tapped out a message, reminding them not to be late for the welcome reception at seven o'clock this evening.

He responded immediately to say they'd meet me in the lobby a few minutes before the function began.

The reservation agent returned at the same time as the man who'd been booked into my room.

"My supervisor found a solution," the agent said, looking at Blue Eyes. "We'll put you in another room tonight and—"

"I hope you're not going to tell me that I have to move tomorrow," he said, his tone strident.

Her skin flushed, and she mumbled, "Um, no sir." "Good." This, from him.

She handed me the room key and reeled off a spiel about the hotel which I half listened to while distracted by Blue Eyes, who'd taken out his phone again.

Check-in complete, I wheeled my suitcase with the duffel bag on top of it toward the elevator. While I waited for it to come, my phone vibrated in my handbag. Before I could reach for it, the elevator dinged, and I decided whoever it was could wait.

I got inside the stall and pulled out the phone.

A hand appeared and stopped the doors from closing. Blue Eyes stood in the doorway. His magnetic gaze captured mine and my heart pulsed to an irregular rhythm.

"Hello, again." He stepped over the threshold and wheeled his suitcase inside, sucking the air out of the tiny space.

His presence wasn't threatening, but my mouth refused to open. I nodded in response to Blue Eyes' greeting and waited for my heart to act right. After a deep breath, I forced my gaze back to the phone.

Angelica, my daughter, had sent me a text. She was seven, super-bright, and had her own phone. I didn't approve of her having it, but her father—the sneaky bastard that he was—gave it to her for Christmas.

Angel was responsible for teaching my mother half of what she knew about her laptop, phone, and tablet. As young as she was, Angel figured out things about my electronic gadgets that mystified me—and I wasn't a slouch.

"This child is something else," I murmured.

Still smiling, I looked up and locked gazes with he-of-the-unkempthair-and-startling-blue-eyes. Frowning, I focused on him. He wasn't as young as I first thought. The overall impression from all that hair and his devil-may-care appearance was that of a youthful, carefree individual.

On closer inspection, Blue Eyes had some age on him. In my thirtyfive-year-old estimation, he was a bit over thirty, but it was hard to tie down his exact age. The slight creases around his eyes, plus the depth to his gaze, told their own story.

"Dammit." His attention went to the phone in his hand.

The elevator stopped, and a couple walked inside.

Where we stood, in opposite corners, didn't necessitate movement and the stall continued upward in silence. When the doors opened again, it was my turn to exit.

Blue Eyes walked out behind me, but we went to opposite ends of the corridor. My thoughts left him when I slid the plastic card into the lock and entered my room.

A narrow passage opened into a tiny living area, a no-frills bathroom, and a spacious bedroom. The furnishings were ultra-modern, and the sheet and drapes came from matching fabric in shades of cyan, hunter green, and teal. I shivered, as the sub-zero temperature hit me, then switched off the air-conditioner.

After turning on the television and flipping through the stations, I settled on a news channel. While unpacking, I hummed to a love song I'd heard on the radio earlier in the day.

On the bed, I spread the dress I was wearing to the reception. I didn't want to be over or underdressed, so I settled on a slinky, black number that complemented my curves and stopped at mid-thigh.

I'd traveled light with the intention of getting some shopping done, but I had enough clothing to get me through the week. Most of the sessions would probably bore me to tears since I wasn't into the nuts and bolts of animation, but I had to put in an appearance and attend the meetings and workshops that pertained to the business side of things.

I wasn't looking forward to spending a week in Miami, not when Angel would be on midterm holiday from school once Ash Wednesday hit this week. Our operations at the office weren't rigid, so if I was in Jamaica she could have spent part of the afternoons with me there.

While my job wasn't wildly exciting, it provided a good salary and my time was flexible. Primrose Goins, my boss, was a no-nonsense business woman but also soft-hearted when it came to family.

That thought was my cue to talk to my lifesaver, so I sat on the bed and dialed Mom's number.

She picked up after a couple of rings. "You're settled in your room as yet?" she asked.

"Yes, I'm about to get ready for the reception."

Angel yelled 'hello' in the background, which brought a smile to my face.

"We're okay here. It's popcorn and a movie for us girls tonight." Mom chuckled, then continued, "I'll let you talk to Angel before she dislocates my arm to get the phone."

"Hi, Mommy." Angel's chirpy tone unknotted the tension in my shoulders. Although she was happy staying with Mom, I worried about shortchanging her whenever I had to travel.

"Hi, baby. I hear you and Grandma are having a party."

"Yeah, we have popcorn and soda—oops. I mean fruit juice."

While she nattered on, I made a note to remind Mom not to go overboard on the soda. Angel was persuasive and half the time, Mom couldn't resist her wheedling when she wanted something.

I looked at my watch and stopped Angel's chatter. "Baby, I've gotta go now. Tell Mom I'll talk to her in the morning."

"Okay, we can talk about the movie when you call."

"Sure thing, honey. Remember to brush your teeth before bed."

"Grandma will help me."

"Love you, baby."

"Love you, Mommy. Muah!" The kissing sound melted my heart and reminded me why I stuck with my well-paying, but sometimes hectic job. Angel deserved everything I could afford and much more. I'd do anything to be home, but that wasn't the case and now wasn't the time to fall into a funk.

The bedside clock told me I didn't have all evening, so I sent off a WhatsApp message to my good friend, Rita, to let her know I was okay.

Almost immediately, she responded with a winking emoticon and the advice to 'get lucky'. We both knew that was next to impossible, so I ignored that advice and threw the phone on the bed.

Within a few minutes, I was in and out of the shower stall. Then, I stood before the mirror applying makeup with a light hand. Most of the time, I used eyeliner and lipstick only and that's what I chose to do this evening.

My hair liked doing its own thing, but I tamed it with a brush, hairpins, and some gel. When I finished, my arms ached a little but the smooth bun I created was worth the extra effort. The eyeliner lent my almond-shaped eyes a bit of mystery and made them appear bigger. The blood-red lipstick and my upswept hair made me look elegant. My only disappointment was my eyebrows that my stylist had threaded with too much enthusiasm. They were now thinner than I liked, but were still presentable.

I shimmied into my dress and slipped into my shoes before going back to the mirror. The rhinestones at the neckline of my dress complemented the diamond studs winking in my ears. The earrings were a birthday gift from my ex-husband.

After spritzing perfume on my pulse points, I rang Joey's room. He and Pete were ready to meet me downstairs.

I picked up my purse and stuck my phone, room key, and lipstick inside it. With a final head-to-toe scan in the mirror, I was out the door and ready to face the evening. The elevator reached the ground floor after only a couple of stops on the way down.

My charges were waiting for me a few feet from the stall. Joey, tall and dark, and Pete, who was light-skinned and plump, greeted and then reassured me they were ready for the evening's activities. Both of them wore dark pants with dress shirts and stood at attention, trying to act older than their twenty years. They were the best of the crop of students sent to us through a government training institution. Joey and Pete enjoyed learning, which made them good candidates to attend this workshop.

On our way to the room assigned for the reception, I listened to Joey's story about a run-in between an older woman and the flight attendant on their way to Miami.

When we stood in the ballroom, a young brunette greeted me with a warm smile. While she checked our names on her list and explained that full registration was scheduled for the following morning, I scanned the area.

My gaze landed on the man I'd dubbed Blue Eyes, and I did a double take. I would have guessed he'd be out of place in this gathering, but I was wrong.

He caught me looking at him and cocked one eyebrow before I could look away. I wasn't about to act like he'd bowled me over, so I allowed a smile to steal across my lips.

That got his attention, and he leaned away from the wall where he'd been lounging and moved toward me.

Read more of this story at this link. https://books2read.com/u/m2l8Zk

Forever Mine

Having loved and lost, can Scott and Shevaughn get things right this time?

After being betrayed by his fiancée, Scott Fine isn't about to trust another woman.

Shevaughn Young escaped from her marriage to a control freak and isn't planning to give up her independence a second time.

A mix up with their hotel booking throws them together and Scott and Shevaughn realize they want the same thing—an interlude with no strings attached.

That's until their connection turns into something they didn't anticipate. Now they're hard-pressed to keep their passion from flaring out of control and into something that looks like forever.

CONTRABAND

Paul drove the thirty miles to Medville in half-an-hour, though the wind from the sea buffeted the Jeep. The royal palms along the coastal road swayed under the fury of the gusts. Mother Nature echoed Mark's rebelliousness.

Someone had moved the white Jeep from where Mark said the accident happened. However, skid marks on the asphalt and a clump of flattened bushes supported Mark's story.

Mark protested when they pulled off the roadway in front of the highway patrol station.

"Why're we stopping here?" he asked.

Paul didn't bother to answer. He got out, rubbed his eyes, and walked into the stationhouse. Grimy spots speckled the blue paint, which ran along the bottom half of the walls. A line of dirt ran parallel to the floor. The top half, painted in white, fared no better. Countless stains marred the walls.

The officer on duty looked up when Paul entered.

"Good night," Paul said.

"Good night. What can I do for you?" the policeman asked.

Mark stood inside the doorframe, arms folded across his chest, and a sour expression on his face.

"My cousin, Mark Weekes, had an accident earlier tonight, with a white Jeep." Paul waved in Mark's direction. "He panicked and ran. I suppose a report was made here, since this is the closest station?"

The bespectacled policeman threw Mark a dark glance before he answered. "Yes. The owner of the Jeep is in the hospital." "Which hospital and how is she?" Paul asked.

"Medville Regional, but I'm not sure what condition she's in."

"Thanks."

The duty officer addressed Mark. "I'll need a statement from you, young man. Come with me."

Mark shifted from one foot to the other before approaching the counter. The officer waved him through the opening to a seat inside, where he wrote down Mark's statement. After forty-five minutes, the policeman asked Mark to read the document and sign.

Paul yawned and stood up when both men walked through the gate in the counter. The officer wore a slight frown and plucked at his moustache. Paul wondered why, but put the fleeting thought aside.

Instead, he asked a question. "The jeep was towed here, I assume?"

"Yes, it's at the back of the yard."

"Can I see it?"

"Sure."

Paul sensed the officer's reluctance to go outside in the biting wind, and guessed he agreed because they saved him the job of finding the hit-and-run driver. Both men exited the front door and went around the side of the building. In the floodlit yard, strong gusts resisted their efforts to move toward the mangled Jeep.

The passenger side looked like crumpled foil paper. The woman barely escaped with her life, Paul thought. He wondered about the extent of her injuries, but didn't allow his face and body language to betray his shock and worry.

Inside, Mark sat where they left him. He didn't acknowledge their return.

"We'll visit the lady in the morning. What's her name?" Paul asked.

The officer's answer was quick. "Miss Phipps."

"Thanks."

When Mark got up, the policeman cleared his throat. "Not so fast, young man. We're not sure what condition Miss Phipps is in, and based on your absconding earlier, you may run off again. I might have to detain you."

Mark stammered his outrage, until Paul quelled him with a look. He sank into sullen silence.

"I don't think you even realize the seriousness of what you've done. It would serve you right if he locked you up tonight." Paul turned to the other man. "Officer—"

"I can turn him over to you," the cop put in hurriedly, "as long as you take full responsibility for him. See that he doesn't disappear like he did this evening."

Paul took his time about speaking. He could be cruel when it suited him, and leaving Mark overnight in jail would give him time to think. He squinted as though deep in thought, holding back amusement while

Mark telegraphed desperate messages to him. Swallowing a nasty smile,

Paul said, "I'll stand surety for him."

The officer motioned to Paul. "Come this way."

Behind the counter, he brought out a form from a battered filing cabinet, filled in the appropriate spaces, and asked Paul to sign.

"When should he report back here?" Paul asked.

"Within the next two days."

Paul nodded, and signed the document, relieved that the policeman hadn't locked Mark up for the night. He could have, considering the nature of the offense.

They didn't talk on the return journey. Paul concentrated on getting them home without falling asleep, while Mark hunched against the door. His resentment sat like a third person between them, but Paul didn't care.

He fell into bed in the wee hours and slept until after midday.

The two-story hospital building sprawled in the center of a manicured carpet of Bermuda grass. In the parking lot to one side of the premises, Paul leaned against the burgundy Jeep. Ten minutes prior, they arrived at the hospital, but Mark insisted he heard an unusual sound from the vehicle. He still tinkered under the bonnet, which irritated Paul since the Jeep ran perfectly.

"Am I going to have to drag you inside?" he asked.

Mark grunted and closed the hood. "No."

Paul shook his head and walked away, leaving Mark to trail behind as he crossed the parking lot and entered the building. Mark hung back when they approached the information window. "Lord, it reeks in here."

"Good morning," Paul greeted the small, bird-like woman inside the space overrun with paper. "We're here to see Miss Phipps, but we're not sure which ward she's on. She came in last night. Car accident."

"Give me a moment please. Let me check." She slid her glasses up on her nose and moved behind the monitor on the counter. After hitting a few buttons, she came back to the window. "She's on Ward E. Are you a relative?"

"No."

She handed him a clipboard. "Write your names and sign here."

Paul complied, and listened while she gave directions to the ward. She handed him two plastic cards with clips attached. "Turn these passes in at the security post when you're leaving."

Paul thanked her and left the counter. They found the ward with no trouble, and the nurse on duty told them where to find Miss Phipps. Paul hid a grin at Mark's attempts to keep his eyes away from the patients. They stopped at the foot of the second to last bed in the airy ward, which smelled of rubbing alcohol and disinfectant. The woman propped up in bed had a thick bandage above her right eye. She studied them with open curiosity. The female in the next bed didn't look away from them once.

Paul smiled at her briefly, and then focused on the person he came to see.

"Miss Phipps?" he said.

Her eyebrow cocked in a questioning arch. "Who wants to know?"

"Paul Weekes. This is Mark Weekes."

She folded both arms across her stomach. "And?"

Paul nodded toward Mark. "My cousin hit your Jeep last night." "And left me in a ditch. Unconscious." She glared at Mark.

Mark slid his hands into his pockets, and examined his shoes.

"Were it not for the kindness of a stranger..."

Mark shuffled, but kept his eyes on the terrazzo tiles. The woman in the bed continued to cast killing looks at him.

"You made him come, didn't you?" she asked Paul, drilling him with a sharp stare. Paul's brows pulled together and before he could voice any thought, she smirked. "I thought so."

He cleared his throat. "The repairs to your Jeep—"

"Yes?"

"I'll pay for those."

"Of course."

Behind his blank expression, Paul's thoughts churned. Did she know how fortunate she was? Mark wouldn't have been easy to find if he hadn't decided to make him face what he'd done. And she could have died. Considering everything, she could be a little less abrupt and a bit more gracious.

Clad in a powder blue duster, with her hair scooped on top of her head, and a pout on her lips, Miss Phipps reminded him of a petulant little girl. She surveyed him out of almond-shaped eyes surrounded by spiky lashes. While he examined her, her teeth worried her lower lip.

Their gaze held for untold seconds. Heat flared in his chest and spread downward. He chided himself over his uneasiness. Her annoyance didn't bother him, but her ingratitude did.

Though he found the situation corny, something connected him to her. She appealed to him—exotic and feisty best described her.

He figured the color of his eyes mesmerized her. It wouldn't be the first time he'd gotten that reaction. Pity he wasn't in any position to explore the interest he saw in her eyes.

When she forced herself to look away, he hid a smile. If they weren't careful, the attraction humming between them would set the sheets on fire. He put aside his discovery while they exchanged contact and insurance information.

He was relieved to find her doing so well, and though not seriously injured, she was staying in the hospital for another day. Thankfully, Mark would only face a fine for driving without a license, and be charged for leaving the scene of an accident.

Paul sometimes worried that a day might come when he couldn't get Mark out of trouble. He hoped the future didn't provide such a test. As things stood, he was obligated to cover the bill for Miss Phipps' car repairs and hospital stay. Plus, he needed to find a way to make Mark pay for this episode.

At the nurse's station, Paul glimpsed a familiar figure. He was not accustomed to seeing the man out of uniform, so it took him a few seconds to recognize the police sergeant. His annoyance grew, and he decided not to acknowledge him, but Sarge turned away from the desk and held out his hand. "Mr. Weekes."

Paul ignored the gesture, but acknowledged him. "Sarge."

Sergeant Singh's skin darkened, his eyes narrowed, and his outstretched hand dropped and curled into a fist. Paul didn't miss the cop's reaction to the deliberate slight, but did nothing to make amends. Greed would be the death of Sarge. Let him work that one out, Paul thought.

"I'll call you," Sarge said in the taut silence.

Paul continued toward the exit, with Mark trotting alongside to keep up.

"Wait up, man." Mark struggled to breathe evenly. "You have a fire to put out, or something?"

Paul slowed his steps, marshaling his thoughts. He was in for some trouble. Sarge's increasing demands for money over the past month had become an annoyance. Paul planned to cut him from his payroll. The trouble was, the policeman would fight to milk the last drop out of the cash cow he thought he had in his grip.

Read more of Contraband at this Universal Link.

Contraband

As master of his destiny, Paul Weekes does what is necessary to survive

He makes his own fortune, but his luck changes when hijackers target his illicit shipments. He has no proof, but suspects the police officer who facilitates his exports off the island of Xantrope has turned on him. To make things worse, Paul's ne'er-do-well cousin is accidentally involved in a gang murder, and a hit is put on him. A budding romance with the cop's niece adds more complication.

Janine refuses to accept Paul's way of life, but inadvertently becomes a victim of his lifestyle. Thrust into kidnapping, double cross and murder, Paul must choose between a relationship with Janine and staying alive long enough to change the course of his future.

DISSOLUTION

Sherryn wanted to close the door on the proof of her husband's infidelity, but there was no going back.

She avoided looking at the child in front of her, whose cupid's bow of a mouth and tawny eyes confirmed that he shared the same genes as her children. But the similarity ended there —his ashy skin, underweight body, and wash-worn clothes pointed to a lack of concern for his well-being and appearance. The woman with him smiled—a smug grimace that deepened Sherryn's suspicion.

She didn't hide her distaste at the sight of the snug tank top holding in

a belly about to surge out of control, or the denim skirt that did little to cover a pair of lumpy thighs. A lustrous, blonde weave complemented the woman's caramel complexion, and false eyelashes emphasized the spite in her gaze.

A quick scan tagged her as the stereotypical product of one of Kingston's ghettos. For timeless seconds, Sherryn felt as though she was stuck in an early 1900s silent film. The wind stirred the flowers and shrubs in the front yard, dried leaves blew over the lawn, and a car drove by, but she heard nothing.

Then the dancehall queen look-alike pushed the little boy forward, dragging Sherryn back to the unthinkable scene unfolding on her doorstep. "Tell Maurice him can have him pickney."

Sherryn suppressed a shiver by pulling her shoulders back. She stood tall, squeezing the doorknob as a shipwreck victim might cling to a lifesaving piece of flotsam. After a glance at the boy, she whispered, "Oh no, you're not leaving him here."

"You ca'an decide dat. Since Maurice won' take care of him, him can keep him."

The woman dropped a knapsack, and spun away with an exaggerated wiggle of the hips and the jangling of gold-plated jewelry, to saunter down the driveway to the gate, where a marked taxi waited.

Ghetto rat! Why leave her child on my doorstep like unwanted baggage?

The boy's bottom lip trembled and he blinked hard several times. Sherryn's chest heaved, and she struggled to slow her breathing. It wouldn't help either of them if she fell apart. Pressing her lips together to keep her focus, she picked up the threadbare knapsack and touched his shoulder. "Come with me."

She left him sitting on the sofa inside Reece's office.

Over the years, Maurice had been shortened to Reece. The inane thought reminded her that she had spent half her life with a man she doubted she would ever really know, and here again, was proof.

The purpose for leaving the boy in Reece's study was twofold. First, he was hidden from her, as if he didn't exist and second, Reece's world would spin off its axis—just as hers had—to find his secret tucked away in his private space. She hoped the experience turned out to be as gut wrenching and devastating as hers.

In the living room, she perched on the edge of the settee and hugged herself. She tilted her head back and stared at the high ceiling. Then she skimmed the familiar paintings, family portraits and oddments, absorbing all that meant home and family.

Everything she'd invested in her relationship with Reece lay in invisible pieces around her like shattered glass.

Cold and sterile on the inside, she sighed, forced herself to get up and climb the stairs to their bedroom. Once there, she lay down and allowed the tears to fall, searing her sinuses and then her eyes. Other than anxiety over her children when they were ill, and tears shed while watching sad movies, no drama had touched her life.

And now this.

She wasn't sure how much time passed before she heard Reece's Land Cruiser throttling in the yard. He was home on one of his afternoon stopovers. Her heart thumped painfully at the confrontation to come.

She hurried into the bathroom to wash her face, staring into her dull eyes before returning to sit on the bed, facing the doorway. She ran an unsteady hand over her close-cropped hair and glanced at her watch, surprised to find that two hours had slipped away since she answered that fateful knock at the door. Briefly, she spared a thought for the boy. He had to be hungry.

Concern fled as Reece bounded up the stairs, calling her name. The door opened, and the energetic man at the center of her world entered the room. He crossed the patterned tiles in a few steps. "Sher, you never hear me calling you?"

She met his eyes, sure her expression would tell him something had gone wrong.

"Sherryn, what happen'?"

She stood up, willing herself not to scream or lash out at him for destroying her near-perfect life. Instead, she said, "It's not what, but who."

He attempted to touch her, but she edged away, ignoring the hurt and bewilderment in his darkening eyes.

"Come downstairs," she said, not waiting to see if he followed.

His footsteps fell heavy on the wooden treads behind her.

Sherryn blinked hard to prevent fresh tears from forming as she turned left at the bottom of the stairs. She paused outside his study and sucked in her belly to pull herself upright. Then she turned the knob on the door and it swung inward to reveal the boy curled up on the settee. He was asleep with a thumb in his mouth.

She pushed sympathy aside and composed herself. Reece's breath bathed the back of her neck, and he grunted in what she supposed could only be surprise.

She faced him and spoke to his pinstripe shirt through the obstruction in her throat. "Don't bother to say anything. I don't want to know."

She brushed past him, and on the way out of the house, picked up her keys from the table in the hallway.

Read more of Dissolution at this Universal Link.

Dissolution

Sherryn Allbright is the envy of her peers. She is a wife, mother, and successful business woman, but her life turns topsy-turvy when a woman leaves a child on her doorstep, claiming her husband is the father.

Denial is useless, for the boy resembles Reece too closely not to be his offspring.

Sherryn is ready to end their marriage and blames Reece's problems on his old neighborhood—a Kingston ghetto. If he'd sever ties there, he wouldn't be caught up in baby-mother drama.

When the boy's mother is murdered, Reece becomes the prime suspect and things go haywire for the Allbrights, whose lives will never be the same.

QUEEN OF KINGSTON

Samantha DaCosta, reporter extraordinaire, stumbles upon an explosive story in her research of several wealthy, humanitarians connected to The Castle, a place reserved for the mega-rich.

Her uncle, who is a member, has invested in a medical facility that produces and distributes vaccines to third-world countries. The medication has deadly adverse effects, which sets up Ted DaCosta as a target for blackmail.

As Sam uncovers disturbing details, she's conflicted. When her personal safety is threatened, she must either pretend not to know the implications of this nefarious plot, or speak up and bring down a hailstorm of publicity. Danger also stalks her to Jamaica in the form of an assassination attempt.

Kingston "King" Coburn is content to support his woman's endeavors, but when work impacts her well-being, he draws the line. Instead of pulling her back from the edge of a dark abyss, he's drawn into the world of power brokers, who will do anything to increase their wealth.

Only the couple's combined skills and access to a safe haven will keep them alive at the end of their harrowing search for the truth.

ABOUT THE QUEENS OF THE CASTLE SERIES

Each Queen book is a standalone, NO cliffhangers

USA TODAY, and National Bestselling Authors have created a world where women can—and will have it all—love, family, career, and leave a legacy while overcoming generational challenges.

These powerful women, brought together for a higher purpose, change lives by providing safety for those who cannot protect themselves; care for those from tragic backgrounds, and make an impact on their families, communities, and the world at large.

The Kings laid the foundation; the Knights created a bridge of hope between continents; but the Queens will change the world.

Book 1–Queen of Lahiana

Book 2–Queen of Shadow Bay

Book 3–Queen of North Shore

Book 4–Queen of Belize

Book 5–Queen of Kingston

Book 6–Queen of Cambridge

Book 7–Queen of Wilmette

Book 8—Queen of Curaçao
Book 9– Queen of Bahia

OTHER BOOKS BY J.L. CAMPBELL

Inspirational Fiction

DNA

Sacrifice

Dominic's Pride

Sacrifice

Romantic Suspense (Island Adventure Series)

Anya's Wish (novella)

Chasing Anya

Contraband

Taming Celeste

Grudge

Hardware

Kings of the Castle

King of Evanston

Knight of Paradise Island

Queen of Kingston

New Adult

Perfection

Fixation

Persuasion

Women's Fiction

A Baker's Dozen-13 Steps to Distraction (novella)

Dissolution

Distraction

Retribution

Absolution

The Thick of Things

The Heart of Things

The Heart of Things

20 Days of Pleasure

Young Adult

Christine's Odyssey

Saving Sam

Short Story Collections

Don't Get Mad...Get Even (free)

Don't Get Mad...Get Even: Kicked to the Kerb

Sweet Romance

The Vet's Christmas Pet

The Vet's Valentine Gift

The Vet's Secret Wish

Cupid's Gift

Sold! (Relative Ties Book 1)

Blindsided (Relative Ties Book 2)

Daycare Santa

Contemporary Romance (Par for the Course)

The Short Game (Par-For-The-Course) Book 1

The Long Game (Par-For-The-Course) Book 2

The Blind Shot (Par-For-The-Course) Book 3

The Spice of Life

Paranormal Romance

Phantasm

9 798230 169741